THE HOUSE THAT HELD SECRETS

J. W. BECKER

The House that Held Secrets

Copyright 2022   J.W. Becker

Published in the United States of America

Dedication

In Memory:

Martin Warta

Michael Warta

John W. Becker

Chapter 1

There were only three weeks left until school was over and summer vacation would begin. Nine-year-old Lucas Carson fidgeted in his seat as Miss Mason, his teacher droned on about the Nixon impeachment. He wondered if the day would ever end. He didn't want to know any more about Nixon. He turned his attention to the school courtyard outside, he had a great view, but the only trouble was that there was nothing going on out there.

"Mr. Carson, are you listening?"

Lucas hadn't been listening, but he knew he needed to give her an answer. "Yes, ma'am."

"Can you tell the class when President Nixon was in office and who was his successor?" She looked directly at him with a stern expression that said he had better know the answer.

Lucas smiled at the teacher; she was definitely the crankiest person he had ever known. It might be because she was so old, she even smelled like dirt. Miss Hilary Mason was a mystery in herself, she seemed to come out of nowhere, right in the middle of the school year and landed in his classroom. Mr. Coffee, their homeroom teacher left for some family crisis and there she was gray hair, funny square glasses, and a long pointer which rarely left her hand. She never smiled and he wondered if she even knew how. She seemed mad about something all the time.

Miss Mason wore dresses that fell to her ankles, he had never seen any another kind of dress on her, so that was why he thought of her as an old lady, she even had on old lady shoes. They were always black, had a slight rise in the heel and tied up the front. He wondered where she got such ancient clothes.

"Mr. Lucas Carson, can you answer the question?"

"Yes, ma'am."

Lucas smiled again and stood up next to his desk. "President Nixon was 37th President of the United States. He was in office from 1969 to 1974 when he resigned because he was going to be impeached. Gerald Ford was his successor, and he gave Nixon a pardon, which in my opinion he didn't deserve."

"Thank you. Now, sit down and pay attention."

The classroom door opened and a screeching voice called out. "Good morning, class. Miss Mason, may I talk to you for a moment."

Lucas groaned inwardly and wonder what he did wrong now. Principal Mrs. Bertha Lytle, also known as the Dark Mistress of Doom, this is what the kids called her, came in and looked directly at him. She smiled in that evil way she had about her. He was waiting for the wrath of the Dark Mistress to descend upon him when he noticed a girl standing slightly behind her.

The teacher and the principal stood together for a few minutes whispering to each other. The young girl stood there waiting.

"Children, this is Savanna Shepard. She has transferred from Atlanta to the Thomas Memorial grade school. I realize that we have only three weeks left in school, but y'all need to welcome her."

There were murmurs of welcome throughout the classroom. Savanna Shepard was directed to sit down across from Lucas. He raised his hand in greeting and whispered, "hey, Savanna."

"Hey." She smiled back at him.

The bell rang and everyone jumped for the door. Miss Mason yelled, "order in this classroom."

Savanna continued to sit in her seat. Lucas was gathering his books and leaned back against his desk. "Aren't you going home?"

"My daddy said he would pick me up at four."

Lucas looked at the clock it was only 3 o'clock. "Doesn't he know school gets out at 3 o'clock?"

"He's a doctor." She said like that would explain everything to him.

Lucas was somewhat confused. "I heard momma say we were getting a new doctor in town. Why would you ever want to live here?"

"Daddy's from Shelby originally, and after momma passed away, he thought it would be better for me and my brother, Colton, if we lived in a small town. They needed a doctor here and I guess he got the job."

"Dr. Pierce retired last year and went off to Alabama to live with his daughter. I'm Lucas Carson. Your daddy sure picked the right place because it doesn't get much smaller than Loan Mountains Edge." He looked up at the clock again. "They close up around here about now, and we want to get locked in the school all night. Come on."

Lucas and Savanna sat on the steps in front of the school. "We only have grades K through six here, and then you have to go over to Branford middle school. Where do you live?"

"Prichard Hill."

"The old Lansing place? I know that house. Bobby Joe Lansing lived there and he was murdered back before I was born. They say he got killed on Grissom Hill. The story went that Alice Jean

Lansing, his momma and Alvin, his daddy, had a terrible fight one night and she grabbed up Bobby Joe and left. I think there was a daughter too, but I don't believe I know her name, it may be Amanda. Anyhow, Bobby Joe got murdered and was left down by the river. They figured his momma did it so that his daddy couldn't have him."

"All that happened in our house?"

"I guess so. I can show you down by the river where they found him if you want."

"What happened to the Alice Jean and Alvin?

"No one knows for sure about the mother, Alice Jean. She and the daughter, I think her name was Amanda, anyhow they just seemed to disappear. Our Sheriff, Johnny Bill Dustin search for them, but he never found them. Mr. Amos Lowery, he owns the Feed and Grain, told me about it. He has to be the oldest person in Loan Mountains Edge. Some say he's over a hundred years old, and with all those wrinkles in his face, I tend to believe it.

"But what happened to Alvin?"

"Oh, he hung himself. There he was just swinging back and forth on the rope, right from the banister in the upstairs hallway. He went all the way downstairs, his feet just above the floor, they never touched."

"That would've really scared me."

"They say that Mr. Lansing's dark brown hair turned from brown to white that day."

Before Savanna could answer a car pulled up and beeped. She jumped up and ran to the driver's door. Lucas watched as a big man stepped out of the car and walked towards him. He had to be over 6 foot tall. The sun glinted off of his sandy brown hair as he strolled towards Lucas. The man took off his sunglasses and piercing blue eyes smiled at him. He extended his hand, Lucas for a moment hesitated before he grasped the hand.

"I'm Jackson's Shepard, Savanna's father."

"Lucas Carson, sir, pleasure to meet you.

Jackson smiled at the boy and reflected that this kid had the bluest eyes he had ever seen. They contrasted greatly against his dark black hair. A small hand yanked at Lucas's shirt.

"I'm Colton Shepard."

Lucas looked down at the little boy. Six-year-old Colton Shepard grinned back at him. He had sandy brown hair just like his father's.

"Hey, Colton Shepard." Lucas said to the little boy.

"You kids run out to the car. I'll be happy to drive you home, Lucas."

"Got my bike your, sir."

"No problem, we can put it in the trunk."

Chapter 2

Jackson's Shepard looked up from the medical book he was reading. "How was school today, sweetheart?"

"Okay, daddy."

Jackson put the book down and pulled Savanna onto his lap, he folded her into his arms and kissed the top of her head. "What's wrong?"

"Daddy, please call me Sandy instead of Savanna. It sounds like a porch on some old mansion."

"I forgot. What's up?"

Sandy ducked her head and leaned against his shoulder. "I guess I just missed momma. She should have been here today to go with me."

"I know. I miss momma too."

"Colton cries sometimes."

"It's hard for all of us, but we'll manage somehow. We're family and we will always be together."

"You won't go away and die like momma did, will you?"

"I'm not going to die. You and Colton are stuck with me forever."

"Are you sure?"

"I'm positive."

~~~
~~~

Mary Shepard was only 27 years old when she died. Sandy was six and Colton three. Jackson had put in a 48-hour rotation at Kingman Hospital in Shelby, Georgia. He was dead tired when he drove up to his apartment. He was glad Sandy would be at school because he really needed to get some sleep and she was always full of questions about his day at the hospital. If he was lucky, Colton would be down for a nap and he and Mary could sneak off and get a couple hours sleep together.

Jackson got out of the car, stretched and grabbed his coat from the back seat. It had been unseasonably cool the last few days. He was so tired he wondered if he would even make it to the door. He could fall asleep right here next to the car.

The minute Jackson walked into the apartment he knew that something was very wrong. He could hear Colton screaming, he dropped his coat and medical book, ran into the kitchen and found Colton in his high chair, red-faced, kicking and screaming.

"Mary." He called out. There was no answer. "Mary."

Jackson went over to Colton and picked him up. The child quieted immediately.

"Hey buddy, where's momma?"

The baby threw up his arms. "Away."

"Away, huh."

The apartment wasn't very big, only two bedrooms, a kitchen and a Great room. He walked through the Great room and was instantly alarmed by what he saw.

The room looked like someone very angry had torn it up. Even the television had been pushed over. The couch was tipped onto its side and all of the quilts were torn and thrown around. The children's toys had been smashed. Every crayon in Savanna's box had been broken in half. They lay next to Mary's prized stained-glass lamp that was in pieces. Colors of red, green, blue, and yellow glinted up at him.

"Mary." He called.

Jackson hurried through the room and over to the bedroom. He still had Colton in his arms when he stepped into the room. He saw her immediately and put his hand over the baby's eyes as he backed out of the room.

Jackson pounded on his neighbor, Mrs. McCloskey's, door. From inside he heard her call. "I'm coming."

When she opened the door, he shoved Colton into her arms. "I'll be back for him."

"What?"

"I can't explain now." He called as he ran back to his apartment.

Jackson walked into the deadly quiet of the apartment and hesitated before going over to the bedroom. Mary lay motionless next to the bed. She was face down in a pool of blood, he reached over to feel for a pulse. He knew she was dead, but felt he had to make sure. He slowly walked back to the kitchen, picked up the phone and called the police.

~ ~ ~

Jackson pulled himself away from the thoughts of Mary and the senseless murder, a murder that had never been solved.

He smiled at his daughter. "Tell me about your new friend."

Lucas, he just started talking to me at school. He's really nice and I like him. We're going to walk to school tomorrow. His momma's Miss Sarah, she works at the hospital where you work."

"Sarah Carson?"

"Yes, you know who she is?"

"I think I do."

"Lucas doesn't have a daddy. He died a long time ago and he doesn't even remember him. I guess I'm lucky because I got to remember momma."

"You'll always remember momma. She will always be with you."

Jackson thought about Sarah Carson. He had met her at the hospital today and she had caught his eye, but he had assumed she was married, and he didn't pursue married women. She had long brown hair and beautiful brown eyes that sparkled when she talked. He thought she was beautiful from the moment he laid eyes on her. She stirred him for some reason, and when he saw her, he realized for the first time that he missed the company of a woman."

"Daddy, are you listening to me?"

"Sorry."

"Is it okay if I meet up with Lucas this weekend?"

"Lisa's coming for a visit."

Sandy slowly moved off of her father's lap. She stood across from him and stared, "how long is she going to stay?"

"Her aunt lives in Barwick about 45 miles from here and she's going to stay with her, and then come over here to visit us. She'll be here for the entire weekend."

"You're sure she's not staying here?"

"No, she will be staying with her aunt."

"Is she your girlfriend now?"

"We're just friends. We've known each other for a long time and she was momma's best friend. You know that."

Sandy screwed up her face. "I remember her from Atlanta. I don't like her too much."

"Why would you say that? She's always been very nice to you."

"She's too nice, daddy, it doesn't seem real. She's nice to me, but not really nice. Oh, I don't know how to explain it to you."

"Did she say something to you that upset you?"

"No, it's just the way she is, always trying to make me like her and......... She tries to be like momma, and she's not."

Jackson pulled Sandy back into his arms. He slowly rocked her back and forth. "Sandy, honey, no one can replace your mother, not in my life, yours or Colton's. Momma was very special to all of us."

Sandy didn't want to talk about Lisa anymore. "I'm really tired, daddy. I think I'll go to bed."

Jackson kissed her cheek. "Good night, baby, I'll be up in a few minutes to tuck you in."

Chapter 3

"Hurry it up, Colton, or we'll be late."

Colton moved slowly behind his sister. He stopped to look at everything. Sandy went back and pulled him away from the snail he was examining. "Hurry up. Don't play with snails. They're nasty."

"They're not nasty, they're just slow."

"Yeah, and if we get any slower were never going to make it to school."

"Who cares?"

"Daddy will wear you out if you don't get your butt to school."

Colton stopped and sat down a large boulder. He reached down to tie his shoe and looked up at the sky.

"What are you doing now?"

"Thinking."

"Walk and think at the same time."

"I can't. It will get away from me."

"Hey." Lucas called running down the road to catch up to them.

"I'm glad you're here. Maybe you can get Colton to move faster, or we aren't ever going to get to school today."

Lucas threw down his books and sat down next to Colton who appeared to be staring at the sky "what are you doing?"

"Thinking."

"About what?"

"I don't want to go to school today."

"Your six, you're not supposed to think that way until you're at least 10."

"Maybe I'm 10 inside."

"Okay. What do you want to do if we don't go to school?"

"Go down to the river and see the spot you told Sandy about. Where that kid was found."

Lucas thought for a second before he answered. "Okay. I really didn't feel like going to school today either."

"Wait a minute. We can't just take off." Sandy protested.

"Were not taking off. We're taking a mental health day."

"Daddy won't buy that."

"Then don't tell him."

"Just how far is it, Lucas?" Asked Colton.

"It's aways from here. Let's go back to my house and I'll get my pony. He can carry all of us and it's a lot better than walking."

"Just one minute, Colton Shepard, you get yourself to school, and you Mr. Lucas Carson don't encourage him to lay out."

Lucas shrugged. "How about we go on Saturday?"

Sandy shook her head. "Can't. Daddy's friend is coming."

"Lisa? Really? Again?" Colton asked. "I'm running away from home."

"Sounds like you don't like her." Lucas said.

Colton blurted out. "I don't. She's mean."

"Keep walking Colton and you are not running away from home. You don't have anywhere to go."

"Whose mean?"

"Lisa, that's who."

Lucas turned to Sandy, "what is he talking about?"

Sandy abruptly stopped and turned to her little brother. She flicked him on the top of the head. "Keep moving." Then, she turned to Lucas, "Lisa was a friend of my momma, they went to school together. She just showed up all of a sudden after momma died and we can't seem to get rid of her."

"Yeah, she sneaked right into our lives. She's creepy." Colton added.

"Why is she creepy?"

"She's hateful inside."

"What did she do make you dislike her so much, Savanna?"

"Call me Sandy. Savanna is too big."

They walked up to the school entrance and Sandy sat down on the step. The two boys joined her. "I really don't know how to explain Lisa. It's weird. She acts all nice, but there's something else underneath, something not right. Look, we have to go in, come on over Saturday and see her for yourself."

The bell rang and Sandy sighed, "Great. We're late. Lucas, bring your pony, and maybe we can get away for a while. Let's go in, we have to hurry."

The three children walked into school and right into the arms of the Mistress of Doom. The Mistress of Doom cackled at them. "Why are you late?".

"Because Colton is slow. He's always been slow."

Lucas didn't know if Colton was slow, but he shook his head in agreement.

"Get yourselves to class, and you better hope I don't find anyone of you," she shook her finger in each child's face, "coming in late again."

~~~

Colton went over to Sandy's bedroom looking for her. She was combing her hair and saw him in the mirror. She turned around and asked, "what's up?"

"She's here."

Sandy looked at the clock on her dresser. "It's only nine in the morning, what is she doing here so early?"

"I don't know, but Lisa the Horrible has arrived."

"You better not let daddy hear you call her that. You better get dressed and come downstairs."

"If I don't, I won't have to see her?"

"You know you're not going to get away with that. Daddy took the entire weekend off because she was coming here."

Colton's eyes widened, "the whole weekend? She's going to be here the whole weekend?"

"Yes. You didn't expect her to come all this way for only a day, did you?"
~~~

Colton fingered the things on Sandy's dresser. "Maybe she'll break a leg or something and go away and never come back."

"You know that won't happen. Go get dressed. Lucas is coming over later so at least we can get away for a while."

When Sandy and Colton went downstairs for breakfast. Lisa was already there. She was sitting at the table like she owned the place. Sandy whispered to Colton, "I think I lost my appetite."

Lisa smiled at them. "Good morning, children."

Colton didn't say a word and slipped into his seat at the kitchen table. Sandy mumbled, "morning."

"How are you children today?"

Sandy eyed her. "Lisa, did you come for breakfast? Daddy burns the eggs all the time."

"Sandy." Jackson warned. "I will make breakfast and I will not burn the eggs."

"Good luck with that daddy."

"I was hoping we could spend the entire weekend together." Lisa beamed. "Maybe take in a show, or go to a restaurant. Is there anything you children would like to do?"

Sandy thought she would throw up because Lisa was being so sickeningly sweet. "The only show around here is the Majestic, they show old movies on Saturdays for the kids. Sundays, the Lutheran Church takes over and services are at nine."

Jackson laughed. "We're in a small town, Lisa, not Atlanta."

"Oh, well, what do you do for fun?"

Sandy shrugged. "We kinda watch the grass grow."

Jackson tapped her on the shoulder. "It's not as bad as all that. Actually, there's a town carnival going on tonight. I thought we could all go to it."

Lisa felt her stomach turn. The last thing she wanted to do was go to some hick carnival in some stupid hick town. She couldn't understand why Jackson had moved to this archaic place! A movie theater that doubled as a church on Sundays, she thought that went out 50 years ago.

Lisa wanted Jackson since she was 13 years old. She had met him through Mary. She stuck close to Mary, hoping to get closer to Jackson, but he had married her. She tried to get over him, but it didn't happen. She was desperate to have him. She admitted to herself that it wasn't love that motivated her, she wanted him because he was good looking, rich, (that was his most appealing quality), and she thought right now, vulnerable.

Mary had been murdered many years ago and poor Jackson had come home to find her. It was a horrific scene, blood everywhere. She started her campaign to squirm her way into his life immediately. On the day of Mary's funeral. She stood by his side, held his hand, and consoled him from the very beginning. She was trying to get closer to his kids, but she knew they suspected something. She had been working on the kids for almost 3 years, and now it was time to push harder. She was tired of waiting.

Her plan was to get him to marry her, get his money, and move him back to a big city, maybe New York. He could practice medicine there and make a lot more money. She wanted a wonderful life, maybe in the Hamptons. She wanted that kind of life and she was going to take him with her. He was her financial means to do it. She knew that Jackson Shepard could make a lot more money if taken in the right direction, and she wanted money.

First thing she would do after they were married was to ship those two nasty kids of his off to private schools, maybe a nice foreign country where they couldn't come home a lot. She laughed.

"Something you want to share?" Jackson asked.

Lisa snapped back to the presence and away from her thoughts. "Just thinking about how much fun the carnival is going to be."

Sandy rolled her eyes. "Yeah. Right."

Her daddy gave her a look that she knew meant they would talk later about her conduct. She shrugged and went back to her burnt eggs.

Chapter 4

Lucas led his pony, Mac to the small grass area across from the house. There was an old shed there and he stepped into it. He discovered two stalls and a side room that probably had been used for tack and feed. It would need a lot of repairs before it could be used again, if they wanted to get a pony.

He sprinted over to the door and knocked on it, a dark-haired woman answered. Nothing could have surprised him more because he thought Dr. Shepard was a widower.

"Excuse me, ma'am, I'm looking for the Shepard's."

"Hey, Lucas, come on in." Colton yelled from the kitchen. "Sandy should be down in a minute."

"Hey, Colton."

"Did you bring your pony?"

"Mac is outside."

"Would you like to introduce me to your friend, Colton?"

"Oh, yeah, Lisa Fredericks, this is my friend, Lucas Carson."

"Pleasure, ma'am."

"Welcome, Mr. Lucas Carson. It's very nice to meet you."

What a phony. Sandy thought as she walked into the room. "Hey, Lucas."

"Hey, Sandy, are you ready to go?"

Jackson walked back into the kitchen and when he saw Lucas, he smiled, "morning, Lucas. Where are you kids off to?"

"Down to Red Rock Mountain, there's supposed to be a small herd of mustang down there."

"Oh, are you going to pet the little horses?" Asked Lisa.

Sandy looked at Lisa like she had two heads. Colton giggled, but Lucas kept a completely straight face. "No, ma'am. These are completely wild horses and we can't get that close to them." He said slowly, like he was talking to a retarded child.

"Y'all be back here by two. Lucas, we're going to the carnival tonight, would you like to come with?"

"Yes, sir, but I have to call my momma."

"Ask your mother to join us. It should be fun."

"I think she'd like that. She gets tired of just talking to me and Mac."

Lisa wanted to roll her eyes and gag. She couldn't believe that he invited another woman to come along. She was screaming inside, but she put on a smile because she needed to first find out who this Mac was, and maybe this woman wouldn't be a threat to her planned.

"Is Mac your father?" Lisa asked.

"No, he's, my pony. My daddy died in Kuwait."

After he said it. Lisa remembered that he said something about a horse and the name Mac so this woman was still a threat.

Jackson went over to Lucas. He leaned down and said, "I'm sorry, Lucas."

"It's okay. I don't remember daddy. I was only two years old when he died. I have a picture of him. Momma said he was a hero."

"When a man defends his country. He is definitely a hero."

~ ~ ~

Lucas, Sandy, and Colton piled up on top of Mac. The horse was a big black-and-white pinto and took all of it in stride. "You be gentle now, Mac, and y'all hang on."

Jackson walked over to the horse and looked up at Lucas. "Where's your saddle?"

"I don't usually use a saddle. Mac is really gentle, he's just big, you don't have to worry because everything will be okay."

Lucas thought that Dr. Shepard was worried about how big Mac was and if he would throw them off. He knew that that wouldn't happen.

"Be careful. Colton, you hang on."

"I will, daddy."

Lucas turned Mac around and slowly walked to the South. Sandy turned and waved at her father.

"I'm sure they will be fine. It looks like a nice horse." Lisa said, smiling. Secretly, she hoped they would break their necks.

~ ~ ~

"Are you sure Dr. Shepard said I should join you?" Sarah asked for the third time.

"Yes, momma."

"Okay, go take a shower and get some of that dirt off of you."

Lucas looked down at his shirt and pants. "I'm not that dirty."

Sarah pulled her son into her arms. "You smell like a horse."

"Really? I don't smell nothing."

"Shower. Now."

"Okay."

"You'd better hurry so were not late." Sarah looked in the mirror for the fourth time. Her soft brown hair fell to her shoulders, "Well, this is as good as it gets." She pulled on a pair of faded blue jeans and her favorite red shirt. She had on sandals, but as an afterthought she put them back in the closet and got a pair of tennis shoes.

"You look great." Lucas called from the bedroom doorway.

She turned around and smiled at her son. "You always say that."

"Because you do." He walked over and picked up the comb on her dresser. "Momma, you do want to go to the carnival, don't you?"

"Of course, I do. It should be a lot of fun. Last year we had a lot of fun. Don't you remember?"

"Yeah, I remember. We had a great time."

The doorbell rang and Lucas called out, "they're here. Let's go momma."

Dr. Shepard stood in the doorway, he was so tall that he filled most of it, he casually held his Stetson in his hand. He grinned at her. Lucas said, this is my momma, Sarah Carson, momma, this is Dr. Shepard."

"I believe we know each other. Nurse Carson."

"Please, call me Sarah."

"Jackson." He said laughing. "I guess we got that out of the way."

Lucas pointed to Sandy and Colton. "These are my new friends, Sandy and Colton." As an afterthought. Lisa was introduced. She mumbled her hello.

The carnival was held on half an acre of land south of town. Mr. Charles Brown owned the land and every year he allowed the carnival to set up there, he felt that it was good for the town and even better for the children. This is been going on for the last 20 plus years.

The entire field was lit up in bright lights, this year's color was a pale peach. Every year the carnival had a different color light. Music greeted them. Jackson parked his truck outside the perimeter of where the carnival actually started. It looks like most of the town had turned out for the fun.

"Okay kids," Jackson said, reaching into his pocket. He gave each child money. "Sandy, you stay with your brother and Lucas. It is now 4 o'clock and we will meet right back here at the car at 7:30."

"Okay, daddy." Sandy said.

"I'll take care of them." Lucas laughed and ran towards the lights. "This isn't my first carnival."

Jackson waved at Lucas. "Good man."

Lisa acted horrified, "are you sure that you should let them go alone?"

"This is not Atlanta and they will be perfectly safe."

The children ran into the crowd while Jackson, Lisa, and Sarah made their way over to the food tent. He grinned at Sarah and said, "ladies, what would you like?"

Jackson picked up and handed them each a paper plate and ushered them through the line. He was greeted by many of the towns people who were serving the food. Although he had been in town only a short time it seemed that most of them knew him.

They sat down at a table and Lisa immediately put her hands around Jackson's arm to show Sarah that he belonged to her. Sarah smiled to herself, the woman was really insecure, she hardly knew Jackson Shepard.

Sarah reflected that she really didn't know much about Dr. Shepard. He was the talk of the town and around the hospital because he was new, good-looking, and single. Word that his wife was murdered had gotten around quickly, a murder that had never been solved. He had two children, Savannah and Colton. The house they lived in had its own mysteries that also included a murder. The townspeople often referred to it as 'the house that held secrets.'

Sarah realized that Jackson had spoken to her. "I'm sorry, I was off in my own thoughts."

"I asked how long you've lived in Lone Mountain?"

"All my life, a local, I grew up here and married a local boy, James Carson. He died when Lucas was very young, and he barely remembers him. I went to nursing college in Atlanta, but came back as soon as I could. After I finished nursing school, I got a job at Jefferson Memorial. End of story."

"You didn't want to stay in Atlanta?"

"No, there were several reasons. Stability for Lucas. My parents were taking care of him for the six months I needed to finish my degree. My momma and daddy are here and momma isn't well anymore. It was hard for her, even for that short time that I was gone to care for Lucas. I tried to come home every weekend to help. Now, they need my help, so I'm glad I'm here."

To Lisa's annoyance Jackson laughed, "short version, huh?"

"Very short."

"Well," Lisa interrupted. "Jackson and I came from Atlanta and we've known each other for like .... Ever!" She drew out that last word.

"Jackson jumped in and said, "Lisa was my wife, Mary's, best friend. We've kept in touch."

Lucas, Sandy, and Colton were enjoying the lights, games, and rides at the carnival while Sarah was trying to be civil to Lisa. The woman was annoying at best. She was constantly touching Jackson and leaning against him. Sarah got the message. Hands off. She found that being in her presence was uncomfortable. She even felt that Jackson was uncomfortable as he moved in his chair. He had gently taken her hands off of him several times.

Sarah got up from the table and said, "I think I'll go find the kids. I'll meet both of you later at the entrance."

"Sarah, don't leave." Jackson called after her. She shrugged; she didn't want to be in this woman's presence one more minute. She waved and disappeared into the crowd. Jackson got up and grabbed Lisa's hand, and then dropped it. "Come on, were going to find the kids."

For reasons he didn't understand he suddenly felt uncomfortable with Lisa's presence also. She seemed way too clingy and he was enjoying Sarah's company. He also knew that she left because of Lisa.

"The kids will meet us, let's stay here together." Lisa whined.

"Lisa, I'm going to find the children, you can come or you can stay here and I'll come back for you."

Lisa wasn't going to leave Jackson along with Sarah. She called after him, "no, wait. I'm coming with you."

Jackson spotted Sandy and called to her. She turned, waved and called Lucas and Colton. "Hey, daddy. Is it time to go home?"

"As soon as we find Lucas's momma. She went looking for y'all."

"Not a problem, Dr. Shepard."

Lucas pulled out his cell phone and called Sarah's number. She answered immediately. "Lucas, where are you?"

"Over by the Ferris wheel. Come over. Were all here."

"Good job, Lucas."

"Thanks, Doc."

Jackson thought the ride home was nothing less than a disaster. Lisa talked nonstop about what a wonderful life they had in Atlanta. Every sentence she spoke was directed at him or herself. He was relieved when they reached the house.

Lisa waited until Sarah and Lucas went home. He was irritated with her because he wanted to have some more time to get to know Sarah better. He enjoyed her company. Tomorrow was Sunday and Lisa would be back in the morning. It had been a lot. It would be a long weekend.

As Lisa drove home, her mind was racing. She realized that things didn't go well this weekend and that had to change. Where the hell did this damn Sarah woman come from? Well, she wouldn't worry about it unless she had to. She could deal with her. She smiled. It wouldn't be the first time that she had to take care of a problem.

Chapter 5

Jackson's office was in the next building adjacent to the hospital. The medical building housed six doctors, radiology, laboratories, and physical therapy. His office was on the first floor, hours 11 AM to 6 PM.

Jackson's nurse, Sally Denton, age 44, had worked for him since the day he opened his practice in Atlanta. After long discussion she decided to move to Lone Mountain's Edge with him.

They were a team; she could handle everything within the office and more importantly, they were comfortable with each other. He also hired two other employees, Eva Crystal, and Ethel Brown. Eva was the receptionist who manned the front desk while Ethel handled all of the insurance and finances for the office.

Jackson walked into the office and was surprised to see Sarah Carson sitting in the outer office. He stood for a moment and studied her. She was beautiful, her brown eyes twinkled as she went through the magazine she was reading. He definitely wanted to get to know her better.

He walked over and asked, "are you here because you're sick?"

Sarah looked up and smiled, "no, nothing like that. I didn't realize that your office hours were this early or I wouldn't have come at all."

Maybe we should continue this discussion in my office. Sarah followed him down the hall to his office. He went to the other side of his desk and leaned back against the wall.

"Is there a problem?"

"Yes."

Jackson couldn't have been more surprised, what kind of problem could there be? "Sit down and let's talk."

Sarah couldn't help but giggle. "Don't look so serious. I just wanted to tell you I had a good time at the carnival and would like you and the kids to come over for dinner. The problem would be if you said no."

Jackson chuckled and took her hand in his. "I would love to have dinner with you, but why don't you and Lucas come to my place. I've got a brand-new grill that I can hardly wait to use."

"We'd love to help you break in your grill. I'll bring the dessert."

"Is tomorrow night alright? I'll have to do some moving of boxes so that we can even sit down."

"How long have you been here?"

"Five weeks. I had to set up the office first. The kids are at least organized, but I only have a bed in my room. We did their bedrooms first."

"No problem." I can sit on a box."

~ ~ ~

Sarah and Lucas arrived at 6 o'clock sharp. Sandy opened the door. "Hey, y'all, daddy's in the kitchen, hopefully he won't burn everything."

Sarah shook her head, "maybe I better go check on him."

"Good luck. Watch out for the boxes, they're all over."

"Momma said were barbecuing, so she brought a salad, and chocolate cake."

Colton beamed as his eyes got big, "chocolate cake?"

"Chocolate cake."

Sandy giggled. "At least daddy can't burn salad, or chocolate cake."

Everyone piled onto the back deck. Jackson had the grill lit and Sarah said she would do the cooking. The three kids cheered.

Jackson turned around and grinned at them, "thanks a lot."

They all had a good dinner together and not one cheeseburger had been burnt. Colton sat at the table licking his fingers. "That was great. Daddy, you should let Sarah teach you how to cook."

"Maybe I will." He turned to Sarah, "It would be my pleasure to take lessons from you."

Sandy turned to Sarah, "I have a question for you."

"What kind of question?"

"Well, you have lived here all of your life and should know the truth of what I've been hearing. There has been grumbling about this house's reputation, mostly at school. It's supposed to have a ghost and a bunch of people died here. Is it haunted, Sarah?"

"I don't know about ghosts or if the house is haunted," Sarah said, "but I can tell you what I know about the house and what happened here."

"Hold on, it's getting dark. I'll be right back." Jackson came back with several lanterns that he placed on the small table that was surrounded by chairs. He passed out blankets to everyone because the air had turned cool. "We might as well be comfortable while we listen to Sarah's story."

"As the story goes," Sarah started, "the house belonged to Alice Jean Lansing and her husband, Alvin. They had a son whose name was Bobby Joe. I believe he was a teenager at the time, maybe about 13 or 14. There was also a daughter, her name was Amanda and she was several years older. You rarely saw the family and no one is sure where Amanda actually is today. She too could be dead. If she's alive, I think she would be around 28 years old right now. She was maybe 15 when all of this happened. Alvin is dead and it is believed that Alice Jean is also dead. Bobby Joe, the son was the murder victim.

"Momma, are you telling that old Lansing story again?" Asked Lucas.

"Yes, they all lived in this house where it happened."

Chapter 6

Amanda Lansing, who now went by the name of Mandy Sterling, was tired. She was eight months pregnant and had worked the six-hour shift at Daisy's. Daisy's was a breakfast and lunch only restaurant, and she was the cook for the restaurant. The heavy lifting, which she tried to avoid was starting to bother her back. She was going to work one more week, and then take a five-week absence.

There was a frantic pounding at her apartment door. "Okay. Okay, just hold on, I'm coming." She dragged herself out of the recliner that she had just crawled into and cursed under her breath. "Who's there?"

"It's Paul. Open up."

Mandy opened the door and saw a very angry man standing in front of her. "Paul, what are you doing here?"

He didn't answer her as he burst through the door, he slammed it behind him. Paul grabbed Mandy by the shoulders. "Were leaving. Get what you can in the next five minutes."

"What are you talking about? I just got home from work. I'm tired. It was a very long day. I'm not going anywhere."

Paul Stanton turned to face Mandy. He snarled, "I don't want to hear any shit from you. Get your ass moving."

"What's wrong?"

Paul produced a pistol and waved it at her. "I said move and I mean now."

"Tell me what's wrong? What's going on?"

Paul got right into her face and sneered, "you don't have to know what's wrong. I've got to get out of town and I'm not leaving without you. There is no time to talk about this, so get moving."

Mandy had lived with Paul Stanton in the town of Marrow for the last two years. Marrow was 70 miles from Lone Mountain Edge. It was her suggestion that they move here because somehow it gave her comfort to be close to the town, she grew up in. The town where her entire family had died. Mandy put those thoughts away from her. She was going to have a new family now. She and Paul were having a baby, she had already decided on a name, girl, Emma Rose, boy, Edward Michael. She hadn't discussed these names with Paul yet, but she hoped that he would like the names that she had picked.

The apartment they lived in was small, one bedroom, kitchen, living room. You could walk from one end to the other in 10 steps. She thought about when she lived in Lone Mountain. It was a grand house with all kinds of different rooms. They had it built back in the 1920s and it was built huge. There were six bedroom, four bathrooms, a large kitchen and screened in porch off of the kitchen, beyond that was a deck. There were two different ways to go upstairs, one off of the kitchen, and the other off of the large corridor that led into the house. There was a big dining room and a room that her father had used as a study. She always envied him that room because it had the huge fireplace in the corner and was surrounded with books on every wall. In the center of the room, he had his desk where he spent many hours. She thought it was funny that you never knew exactly what he was doing, but as a child, it didn't matter.

She thought about the Great room and laughed. "That damn room was bigger than her entire apartment." There was a beautiful garden in the back. Off of the deck she remembered all the colorful roses that grew every year and came back, year to year. There was a huge basement downstairs that she had played in as a child. She and her brother, Bobby Joe, would play down there on rainy days when they couldn't go outside. There was also the attic. She wondered if it was still filled with all the things that fascinated her as a child, she might never know. Yes, she missed Lone Mountain, and if you could miss a house, she missed that one.

Mandy was brought back to reality when Paul shouted at her. "Mandy, now!

Mandy stepped away from him. She couldn't believe that this was her Paul. Paul, who always treated her like a queen. Paul, who wanted nothing more than to be a father to his child. Paul, who made dinner for her and massaged her swollen feet. She looked carefully at this man she had loved and realized that he was frightened. There was a wild look in his eyes. He held a gun in his hand while pacing back-and-forth across the small living room.

Paul, sit down and tell me what's going on. We'll figure this out together."

Paul walked over to her, raised his hand and struck her across the face. She was off balance and fell to the ground. Her hand flew to her belly. He looked down at her and screamed. "Shut the hell up." He went down to his knees next to her. "You get this straight; I will not leave you behind because that kid inside of you is mine and I intend to keep it. Once the kids born. You can go your way, but it's mine."

Mandy was shocked by his treatment and the declaration that he really didn't want her. All he wanted from her was the child.

"Paul................ "

"Shut up. Just shut the hell up. Don't you understand we have to hurry?"

The door flew open. "Stanton, is the bitch ready? If not............ Leave her. The cops are right behind us."

Paul turned to Mandy; the anger apparent in his face. He tried to jerk her up and growled, "dammit, get your ass up, right now. I don't have any more time to argue with you, we have to go. Leave everything here."

Mandy was standing next to the small fireplace in their living room, she put her hand on it. It was fake, but she loved the fireplace. She shook her head and backed away from Paul.

"Leave the bitch. We have to go right now."

"I want my kid, Stanley. She goes with the kid."

"Get it later after it's born. Paul, you're the one who pulled the trigger on Barton. Do you want to get the chair?"

Mandy moved forward and grabbed Paul's arm, "what is he talking about?"

"Paul!"

"I told you to shut up. All of you shut up. Stanley, Alvin, get out of here. Give me a few minutes."

"Screw this." Stanley yelled and pointed his revolver at Mandy.

Alvin Stanton was Paul's 42-year-old brother. There was an 18-year difference in their ages, but Paul had always been the leader in the group. Stanley Richards was an old friend of Alvin's; they had been together since childhood. When Al Barton, the owner of Barton's jewelry pulled a shotgun from under the counter, Paul was the one who shot and killed him. He put four slugs into his chest before he could get a shot off. As Al Barton lie dying behind the counter, Paul, Alvin, and Stanley Richards cleaned out the entire store of anything of value. They had over $4 million in diamonds and precious stones, plus almost $7000 in cash. It was time to get out of the town of Marrow.

After the robbery and murder, Paul had insisted they go back for Mandy and then he was going to hide the jewelry where no one would find it.

"I'm not going with you, Paul."

Mandy never actually felt the bullet that entered her abdomen because she was thrown backwards against the fireplace and lay unconscious. Paul turned to Stanley; he was furious. He shot her a second time.

Paul grabbed him by the shirt. "What the hell did you do? You killed my kid."

Paul shot Stanley Richards where he stood. One shot to the head and the 265-pound Stanley slumped down without a word. Mrs. Helen Hardly, a 78-year-old widow of 30 years, stood in the doorway of Mandy's apartment. "Just what is going on here?" She demanded. "A person can't hear the television with all of the shouting going on." Mrs. Hardy noticed the still form next to the fireplace. "Oh, my God, Mandy?"

~~~

Mandy and Mrs. Hardly were friends for the two years that she lived here. Mrs. Hardly would often have her over for tea. Mandy enjoyed listening to the stories that the older woman told about her youth. On weekends they would often spend pleasant afternoons together.

Mrs. Hardly had become very involved in Mandy's pregnancy. She had crocheted the baby a soft, blue, yellow, and pink blanket. She made several little outfits with booties to match. They were made in white and each was trimmed, either in yellow or powder
~~~

green. Mandy was touched by the gifts and said she would always treasure them.

Mrs. Hardly also bought a beautiful silver picture frame with engraved baby shoes on the bottom for the baby's first picture.

It was Mrs. Hardly that Mandy discussed names with and went through countless baby magazines showing different items that she would need.

Mandy had come to not only love this old woman, but to depend on her in so many ways for so many things. This was her first baby and she would need help and advice. Mrs. Hardly had raised seven children of her own. Pictures of each one stood on her piano. She looked at them and reminisce about the children as she played her piano. Mandy loved to listen to her play the soft music. She had a very special talent for it. Mrs. Hardly said that she didn't play much anymore because of her arthritis, so when she did, Mandy found it very special.

~ ~ ~

Paul had shot Mrs. Hardly in the chest as she went to help Mandy. He stepped over her without concern, went to the fireplace and leaned down to check if Mandy was still breathing. "She's dead, Alvin, the son of a bitch killed my kid."

Alvin went over to his brother and looked down at Mandy. "We can't change this; we need to get out of here. The cops are on our trail, and should be here any minute. You can't do anything for her."

Paul took one last look at Mandy before he left. He went out the back door and down the stairs to where they had left the car. When they got to the car, Paul started to laugh.

"What's so funny?" Alvin asked.

"Probably the best that they both died. What the hell would I do with the kid. Let's get out of here while we can."

Chapter 7

It was just dumb luck that they had gotten away before the police came. Paul decided that they had to hide the jewelry and come back for it later. His reasoning was that if they got stopped there would be nothing to connect them with the jewelry store murder. He would also hide the guns that they carried because it was easy enough for him to get other guns.

Paul remembered that Mandy had lived in Lone Mountain Edge. He even remembered the address because he had found it funny. 1616 Mockingbird Lane. He would kid her that one day she should just fly back to the Mockingbird.

When his brother objected, he told him that it wasn't that far to Lone Mountain and he had the perfect spot to hide everything. It took him a little over two hours, it was dark and that was perfect for them. They went to the house and sat outside for another hour, when there was no activity, Paul went to the porch and rang the bell. There was no answer. He jimmied the lock and went inside, it was empty. Whoever lived here wasn't here now, and he felt the urgency to hurry before they came home. There were boxes all over, which made him think that someone was just moving in. It really didn't matter because he could get rid of a problem if he had to, he hoped that no one came home while he was there. He felt the gun in his pocket and was reassured.

Paul found the stairs that led to the attic, he slowly opened the door and went up. He found it full of all kinds of oddities. Old furniture, boxes marked for Christmas, toys, knickknacks of all kinds, several old televisions and dressers. There were a lot of dressers. He looked around; it was just as Mandy had described it to him. She said that her brother used to play up here with her. They also played in the basement, but she had preferred the attic.

Paul searched for the additional room Mandy told him about, he found it behind one of those old dressers. He pulled the dresser away from the wall and felt for the small button she said was at the bottom. Once he found it, he pushed and the door snapped open. Inside was a 4 x 4 room with a small table and chairs. In each chair, a rather large doll sat as if waiting for someone to come and play with it. A tea set was in front of each doll. There was even a pink hanging light over the table. He searched for a switch and found one, the light switched on and gave off a soft pink glow.

Paul laughed when he saw that there were even more dressers in this small area. He stepped forward to open one of the drawers and felt a depression underneath his foot. He went down to his knees and felt along the floor. The floorboard was loose. Paul took out his knife and carefully prided it up. There was just enough room for both the jewelry and the money. It would do just fine and a perfect place to hide them. He worked as quickly as he could and secured the jewelry, the money, and the two pistols. He pressed the boards back down and retraced his steps until he was on the main floor. There actually wasn't much room up there with all of the stuff that had been stored. He smiled to himself, because no one would know that he had even been here.

~~~

Detective Lenny Gardner was the first on the scene. He had beaten the black-and-white. Several residents of the building were gathered around Helen Hardly's body.

Davis Harris, who was the next-door neighbor said, "I think she's still alive. I called an ambulance."

Within minutes, the responding black-and-white arrived, along with the ambulance. The lab techs and coroner were close behind
~~~

them. Mrs. Hardly was placed in the black bag reserved for the dead and zipped up tight. Mandy was stabilized and sent to the hospital emergency room, they had to go the 70 miles over to Lone Mountain Edge because Marrow was even smaller and had no hospital.

Lenny Gardner slowly walked around, this was definitely a no-frills, apartment, he sighed and started his investigation. Patrolman Michael Brackett handed the detective a lighter he found next to Mandy. "It's initialed P. S.; The lady was eight months pregnant, took the bullet in the lower abdomen and shoulder. Do you think the baby's death?"

"They're probably both dead."

~~~

Dr. Shepard was the emergency room physician on call when Mandy arrived. She was unconscious, her condition at best was seriously guarded. He immediately had her taken to an exam room where he placed her on additional IVs and examined her wound. She had been hit in the lower abdomen. He saw no exit for the bullet.

Sarah was working the Emergency Room with Jackson, he turned to her, "Call Dr. Albert's down here. This baby isn't going to wait."

Dr. Albert's arrived too late to usher baby boy Sterling into the world. Dr. Shepard had that privilege.

Dr. Shepard held the tiny little soul close to him as he watched his mother being taken away to the ICU unit. He rocked the baby slowly. "He's perfect except for a crease on his butt from the bullet, but that will heal nicely

"Is that the mother?" Dr. Albert's asked.
~~~

"Mandy Sterling, unfortunately, she's in critical condition, not only from the wounds, but from the baby's birth. We had to do a cesarean section to get this little guy out."

Sarah came over to Jackson and he handed her the baby. She looked up at him and grinned, "it's been a long time since I've held one this little. I'm going to take him up to the intensive care nursery."

~~~

Detective Lenny Gardner, and several other detectives were still at the Sterling apartment. They were looking for anything that could help them find the murderer of Mrs. Hardly, and who shot Mandy Sterling and left her for dead. They had found evidence that several people had been in there recently.

Mandy Sterling's purse had given them the information to identify her. Lenny called Officer Bracket over to him. "At least we have a name for the victims. Bracket, which hospital was Sterling taken to?"

"Jefferson Memorial over and Lone Mountain, it's the closest critical care unit around here."

Lenny casually went over to the bedroom where he found several letters that were written to a Paul Stanton. They were laying on the table next to the bed. He picked up the letters and studied them, for some reason the name on them seemed familiar.

Lieutenant Andy Crystal held up a 45-caliber pistol he found in the top dresser drawer across from the bed. "Maybe it belongs to this Stanton guy, or maybe Mandy. If she lives, we can ask her."

They continued to search throughout the apartment, which didn't take long because it was so small. Lenny wanted to go through the apartment again, but Andy was ready to leave.
~~~

"You can stay here and check to your hearts content, I'm going over to the office and check out this Paul Stanton and see if he has any priors. I will also check out Mandy Sterling."

Andy took the evidence bags and headed for the door. He turned back and shouted to Lenny, "meet you back at the 21."

"After I leave here, I'm going over to Lone Mountain and check on this Mandy Sterling first."

"Okay. Later."

After Lenny had completely gone through the apartment one more time. He walked across the hall, the apartment door was wide open and he walked in. He walked over to the piano and looked at the pictures of the seven children on top of it. He checked the mantel of the fireplace and picked up a picture of the dead woman, Mrs. Helen Hardly. She was smiling in the picture and looked like she didn't have a care in the world, and now she was lying dead in the morgue because some asshole shot this defenseless woman. Life wasn't fair.

He carefully went through her entire apartment and found nothing that would help the case. On her chair was a stash of crocheting, he picked it up. A catch of blue, pink, green, and yellow was incorporated into some kind of blanket, it was for a baby.

Lenny sighed, as he looked back at the seven silver framed pictures. He was going to hate to have to notify them that their mother was dead.

Chapter 8

Lenny Gardner walked over to the hospital telephone operator and showed her his badge. "Can you tell me what room Mandy Sterling is in? And also, I need to know who took care of her when she came into the emergency room."

The telephone operator, Marie Toomey, looked at this tall, gray-haired man. He seemed to be middle-aged or maybe a little older, possibly in his 50s. He was good-looking. She smiled at him and said, "Mandy Sterling is in the intensive care unit. I'm afraid you'll have to check with the emergency room to find out who treated her down there."

"Thank you. I'll do that."

"Anytime."

Lenny decided that he would go down to the emergency room first. Sarah asked if she could help him. He produced his badge and explained that he came from the town of Marrow. He told her he was investigating Mandy Sterling's attack. "How is Ms. Sterling?"

"She's in intensive care. Dr. Jackson Shepard took care of her while she was in the emergency room. Would you like me to page him?"

"Please, ma'am. I'll just sit over there and wait."

Jackson went to the emergency room immediately when he heard the page, he walked in and saw Sarah. He gave her a big smile. "Hey, sweetheart. You rang?"

"There's a detective here to see you about Mandy Sterling."

"Really?"

"He's from Marrow. Seems there was a robbery involved with jewels and diamonds. There was also a death." She pointed to the tall man who was slouched in one of the chairs in the waiting room.

"What's his name?"

"Detective Lenny Gardner."

Jackson went over to where Lenny was sitting, his first thought about the man was that he looked tired. "Detective Gardner, I am Dr. Jackson's Shepard."

Lenny got up and extended his hand. "Sergeant Lenny Gardner from Marrow. I came to speak to you about Mandy Sterling."

"Let's walk over to the doctors lounge and I'll buy you a cup of bad coffee."

"Works for me, Doc."

Jackson sat down in one of the soft chairs across from the detective. He took a sip of his coffee while evaluating the man. Jackson cleared his throat. "What can I do for you?"

"We're interested in Mandy Sterling for several reasons. She was shot by persons unknown, and there were two dead bodies in her apartment with her."

Lenny took out his notebook and referred to it. We identified the dead man as Stanley Richards. He's a smalltime thief with an arrest record longer than my arm. We believe he was involved in a robbery at Barton's jewelry store, Mr. Al Barton was killed and several million dollars in jewelry had been taken. There was also six or $7000 in cash.

Ms. Sterling's neighbor, Helen Hardly was also murdered, she was in her 80s. There is evidence that there may be at least two others involved, and there's also the possibility that Ms. Sterling is involved. It is important that I speak to her as soon as she's available."

"Mandy Sterling is in critical condition and in our intensive care unit. Currently she is unconscious. There is no telling how long it will be, or if she will regain consciousness at all. We had to take her baby by cesarean section to save his life. He's in our NICU.

"What are her chances?"

"Not good. The bullets to her abdomen and shoulder did damage, the birth was hard, and she was in shock."

"We looked for relatives, but as of right now there are none, no parents, no siblings, no aunts, uncles, not even a distant cousin. How about the baby? How is he doing?"

"He's doing well. He'll be in the hospital for a few weeks. He was premature and nicked by the bullet. He needs a little help right now. Dr. Elizabeth Jackson is his attending physician. She's on our pediatric service."

Lenny let out a low whistle. "That poor baby, as far as we know, he's alone in the world. Keep him here as long as you can because it's a hell of a lot better than the State Care. Even foster care isn't so great these days. Too many crazies out there."

Jackson nodded. "We'll see what we can do for him."

"Doc, I want these Bastards. I only wish that I could have caught them standing over good old Stanley's body with a smoking gun, but that didn't happen. They shot down an old lady, and she was a very nice old lady with seven children and tons of grandchildren. I could care less if they kill each other because they've already caused so much harm to so many. Please, give me a call as soon as Ms. Sterling can talk." Lenny handed Jackson a card.

"You will be my first call."

Jackson had put in a long day and he was tired, he wanted nothing more than to go home and be with his kids. The page overhead called a code for the second time to the ICU unit. He just knew that the problem was Mandy Sterling. He ran down the hall and bolted into the unit.

They worked on Mandy for two hours. Her heart stopped three times before it had captured and stayed erratic, but steady. Jackson wondered why she was still alive because by all rights, she shouldn't have survived this. He ran into Dr. Henry McMillan on the way out of the ICU unit. He informed Dr. McMillan of Mandy's condition because he was taking over for the evening. Dr. McMillan was a cardiologist that had just been assigned to her case, he went over the records with him before he left. He thanked him and informed Jackson that he would call if there were any changes in her condition.

~ ~ ~

Jackson parked in the long driveway and looked up at his house. He had bought the house, sight unseen because he was desperate to get out of Atlanta. He thought it was a strange house at best, now he found out that it also had a strange history. He shrugged, went in and found everything quiet, too quiet. He looked around and didn't see Sandy or Colton, he wondered what the kids were up to.

"Sandy. Colton."

Sandy popped up from the doorway in the kitchen that led down to the basement. She ran over and gave him a big hug, "hey, daddy. Guess what?"

Jackson threw his keys on the table and slumped down into the chair. "What? I'm just too tired to guess."

Sandy pointed to the door that went downstairs. "There's a whole basement down there and it goes all the way through the house from one end to the other." She sat down on the chair across from him. "Someone………"

"Hey." Colton yelled and pulled out a chair next to his father. He looked over at Sandy, "did you tell him?"

No, not yet. Hold on."

"Guy's, Can I have a cup of coffee with the story?"

"I'll get it, daddy."

"Thank you, Sandy."

Sandy ran over to the coffee pot, put a cup under it, and pushed the button. Jackson got up from his seat, took off his shoes and suit coat before dropping the coat onto the back of the chair, he sat down again.

Sandy went over and undid his tie, something she liked to do. He took her hand and kissed it. "Hang on a minute, daddy, I'll go get the coffee."

"Hurry it up. We've got to show him." Colton yelled.

"Hold on, Colton, daddy needs his coffee first."

"You've got to hurry."

"We've got all evening, son, relax."

The doorbell rang. It was an unnerving ring because it sounded just like the theme from the Twilight Zone.

Sandy cringed. "You've got to change that, daddy."

"I agree. I'll take care of it tomorrow."

"There it goes again."

"Go answer the door, Colton."

"I'm on it."

Colton came back with Sarah and Lucas. He pointed to them, "look who I found."

"Lucas and I are going to dinner and we thought that maybe y'all would like to come with us."

Jackson grinned at her. "I have a much better idea, let's order pizza and put on a DVD."

Sarah looked at Jackson, he not only looked tired, he looked exhausted.

"That sure works for me." Lucas agreed.

Colton shook his head. "Yeah, and then we can show Lucas what is downstairs."

"What's downstairs?" Lucas asked.

"You better let me tell it, Colton."

Sandy turned to her daddy. "I think maybe it would be better if we showed you."

Jackson, Sarah, Lucas, and Colton followed Sandy down the two flights of stairs to the basement. There was a small landing that separated them and Sandy stopped there. She reached up and flipped on a light switch that lit up the entire downstairs.

They went down and walked into a huge room that extended from one end of the house to the other. "Watch." Sandy called as she went to a row of switches at the bottom of the stairs and flipped them on, it lite up the basement even more.

Sarah looked down to the other end of the basement and gasped, "this is incredible."

"Wow." Lucas added. "How big is this? Who did this?"

"I don't know. Colton and I found it this way."

Colton shook his head in agreement, "it's great."

Jackson was examining the paintings that were not only on the walls, but also on the floor. The walls were decorated in bright colors, depicting all types of buildings and establishments. There were houses of every color, a Marshall's office a gas station, bank, Jonas's General Store, and even a post office. The painted buildings ran up and down the entire wall area.

The basement was so large that many of the buildings, the Marshall's office, general store, bank, and post office had been built out and you could actually walk into them. Inside the general store there were shelves filled with food boxes that someone had taped together to make them look real. There were flour sack's that had been stuffed with paper to make them look full. An old barrel with fake apples sat next to the counter where you would pay for your goods.

There was a stove next to another barrel that had a checkerboard on top of it. Two chairs sat on either side of the barrel. The checker game looked like someone had just gotten up and left right in the middle of it.

"This is amazing." Sarah said.

They went into the bank next. It looked like it had just come out of an old western movie. There was a swinging wooden gate that you went through to get to the teller's cage. The drawer held monopoly money. The teller cage was separated from the customers by iron bars. In the corner was a full size safe that stood open.

Jackson went over and picked up one of the gold bars in the safe. It was made of wood and had been painted bright gold. "Now that is amazing."

"Wait until you see the Marshall's office, daddy."

"I love this place." Colton said.

Outside of the Sheriff's office there were three chairs next to the door. A board with wanted posters hung on the wall. Sandy pointed to the one that said William Bonnie, a.k.a., Billy the Kid.

They went into the Marshall's office and found a small desk in the corner, across from it were two cells with cots in them. The thing that impressed Colton the most was the rack of six rifles against the wall, and a holster with a gun that hung on a peg next to the jail cell. Another peg held a Stetson just like Colton's daddy wore.

The guns were toys, but looked very realistic. Outside of the Marshall's office was a hitching rail. Lucas grinned at it and said, "all we need is a horse."

"Jackson, who would've done all of this?" Sarah asked. "It's absolutely incredible."

"We bought this house sight unseen. I didn't know about any of this and the real estate agent, Tony something, never said a word."

"It seems to be a combination of the old West and," she pointed to the other half of the basement, "something more modern."

"Let's go check out the rest of it."

The basement curved at an angle to the left, but they couldn't see what was there because it lay in the shadows. This part of the basement was designed like a street and had a 2-lane highway going from one end to the other. The street was complete with stoplights.

Sandy ran down to the other end of the basement, reached up and threw another set of switches. She pointed at the stoplights, "they work."

They walked down to the end of the basement and Jackson looked to the left, he discovered that there was another side that curved around. The street continued around to this end of the basement. This also had buildings that lined the walls. It came around in a large circle that led back to the stairs and the main floor. Half of the basement was set up as a speedway, and the other like you just stepped into the old west.

Sarah shook her head. "This is incredible. Jackson. You have no idea who did all this?"

"This is the first time that I've been down here."

"There's more." Sandy yelled. "Over in the back here, in that indentation, someone built a garage."

"It's got cars in it." Colton yelled running over to the garage. He flung the doors open.

The garage had a double door on it that opened outward, inside were three cars, they all looked brand-new, one was green, there was also a red, and blue one. Jackson walked in to examine the cars, they were peddling cars, something he had not seen in a very long time. He pulled the red car out, it looked like it had been constructed yesterday. The cars had racing stripes and each had a number. The red one was 32, the green 66, and the blue 47. They were big enough for the kids to get in and the pedal system would allow them to move around the painted streets.

Colton was so excited he jumped up and down. "Can we try them?"

Jackson grinned at the little boy, he thought he would bust if he said no. "Sure, why not, but you have to be careful. Let me show you how they work."

With Lucas's help. Jackson brought out the other two cars and lined them up parallel to the street. Sandy immediately claimed the red one and Colton got into the green one."

Jackson showed them how a pedal car would work. "don't run anybody down and mind the traffic lights."

"Make sure you're careful." Added Sarah.

Sarah and Jackson watched the children for an hour before they decided it was safe enough and left them to go upstairs. Jackson turned and gave Sarah a quick kiss. He grinned at her, "what would you like on your pizza?"

"I'm a purist. Cheese only. Lucas will eat anything."

Jackson picked up the telephone and called his favorite pizzeria, Chuck's place. It was the only pizzeria in town. He ordered two pizzas, an extra-large double cheese, and a cheese and sausage."

"They should be here in about 45 minutes; I also ordered a couple liters of soda."

Jackson led Sarah into what he called the viewing room. He had just had it finished, converting it into a television room so that he and the kids could be comfortable while they watched their favorite movies. He had an 85-inch TV installed on the wall, there was a large couch and three chairs. As an afterthought he had several beanbags scattered around the room.

He added several large, soft blanket throws and fluffy pillows because sometimes he liked to sleep while the kid's watched television. In one corner was an old-fashioned popcorn machine, opposite that was a small red refrigerator that he kept filled with juice and soda.

Sarah giggled, "all we need is a dog."

"Everything is in the quest of comfort. The kids and I often save Saturday nights for movies. It's our way of relaxing."

"Works for me."

"It's also a way for me to get away from the boxes."

"Maybe I should come over and help you."

"Saturday? We could spend the day in the adventure of box's and then have an evening in the television room."

"It's a date."

Jackson and Sarah made themselves comfortable on the couch, he grabbed a red and yellow throw and covered both of them before turning on the television.

Twenty minutes later Sandy was shaking her father awake, both he and Sarah had fallen into a deep sleep in front of the television. "Daddy, the pizza man is here and I need to pay him."

The kids ate pizza, watched a movie and talked about their new discovery down in the basement. They were planning their next races. Colton was fascinated with the western side of the basement. He enjoyed siting in the Marshall's office. He found a drawer that had all kinds of wanted posters and loved looking through them. He also found a Marshall's badge which he now wore everywhere.

When the evening came to an end, Sarah really wasn't ready to leave. She enjoyed being with Jackson and the kids. He surprised her, delighted her, and gave her a feeling of security, something she hadn't had in a very long time.

"Boy, am I in trouble."

Sarah looked over at her son who was sleeping in the passenger seat. He looks so much like his father and only his eyes were like hers, even though they were different colors. She had brown eyes, and his were a bright blue.

Sarah hadn't even thought about another man until she had met Jackson. Jackson, he seemed to consume her, lately it was all she could think of. The very thought of that scared her because she was afraid, she might fall in love with him and she didn't know if she could do that again. None of it made sense to her, and what about Lisa? How did she fit into his life? Was he in love with her? She certainly seemed adamant with him. She clung to him like he was going to run away. She decided she couldn't think about this anymore. She was tired and needed to sleep. She never should have gotten under that blanket with him.

Chapter 9

"Tomorrow is a school day. Y'all need to get to bed now. Sandy, I may be late tomorrow night. Mrs. Dutton's telephone number is next to the phone if you need her, or I can ask her to come and stay with you."

Sandy stepped on the stairway. "Where you going tomorrow night?"

"I've got a date."

"A date? Like, with a real woman type, date?"

Jackson leaned over and kissed Sandy's cheek. "Like, with a real woman."

"Who?"

"Sarah……"

"It's Lucas's momma, isn't it?"

"Yes, Lucas's momma. Do you want me to call Mrs. Dutton?"

"Daddy, I'm not a baby, and I take care of Colton."

"Are you sure?"

"I'm positive."

"I think I'd feel better if Mrs. Dutton came over."

"Okay, she can watch a movie with us."

"Oh, by the way, Lucas will be joining you."

~~~
~~~

Jackson had no intention of leaving Sandy and Colton on their own, but thought it was better if Sandy thought it, was her idea. Sarah was also happy to hear that Mrs. Dutton would be supervising them. She would be coming over with Lucas around 6 o'clock.

It was Friday night and Jackson had made reservations in Ashburn, 15 miles south of Lone Mountain, the restaurant was one of his favorites, Angelo's. With any luck they wouldn't get paged. He had asked Dr. Anderson to take call for him, he said it wouldn't be a problem.

Jackson looked in the mirror and adjusted his tie. From the doorway he heard, "it's perfect, daddy. Sarah and Lucas are here."

"Okay, honey, I'll be right down."

"Oh, and Mrs. Dutton is here too."

Mrs. Bertha Dutton was a retired schoolteacher. She had soft gray hair and the darkest brown eyes that Sandy had ever seen on a person. This was the third time Jackson had used Mrs. Dutton to watch the children. She was very reliable and would come at a moment's notice. If he got stuck at the hospital, she would pick the children up at school. She was available to him with a phone call. She agreed he could call her anytime, day or night. Her son, Russell Dutton was a physician in Marlow, Texas. She understood the demands of the job. He was happy and grateful to have her.

Jackson thanked Mrs. Dutton for coming. The smile she gave him was soft, almost angelic, "anytime, Doctor, I enjoy the children, and even the movies that they pick out. You and Sarah have a good time and don't worry about a thing."

He turned to Sarah; her long brown hair lay softly on her shoulders. She had a wonderful yellow summer dress on, complemented by yellow and white sandals to match. A small spray of white pearls wrapped around her neck. She was beautiful. He smiled and took her hand.

"Let's go, while the going is good. Y'all behave for Mrs. Dutton."

"We will," came the chorus of voices.

"Go." Mrs. Dutton called after them. "Have fun."

Jackson and Sarah drove out to the small Italian restaurant where he had made a reservation two weeks ago in anticipation of asking her out. On the drive. Sarah confessed, "I'm a little nervous."

Jackson raised his eyebrows in surprise. "I make you nervous? Is it the boxes were facing tomorrow because you don't have to help us?"

"No, of course not. Boxes I can handle. Jackson, I haven't been on a date since I was in high school. After Lucas's father died; I was so consumed with, well, life in general because this was the first time, I was going it alone. This is also the first time I'm going out."

Jackson couldn't help but laugh. "It's been a long time for me too. Relax, we're just going to a great Italian restaurant and we're going to have a good time." He grinned at her, "unless you want to go up to Lori's Ridge and neck with the teenagers?"

Sarah giggled, she couldn't help it because the thought of sitting in the car and making out with a dozen other cars around her struck her funny.

"Let's go to the restaurant. We'd probably both wind up in traction if we tried to go up to Lori's Ridge and make out."

~ ~ ~

A dark blue nondescript Chevrolet moved behind Jackson's silver Lexus at a discreet distance. The lights on the Chevy were not on. When Jackson turned so did the Chevy.

The night was dark which helped the Chevy remain undetected. When Jackson turned into the restaurant, the Chevy drove by and continued to go down the road. After they had gone into the restaurant the Chevy turned around and drove back to park across the street. The dark figure inside the Chevy waited patiently behind the wheel. Dressed all in black the person became almost invisible.

After waiting for an hour, the black figure got an idea, put the car in gear and drove away.

"Later." Black figure giggled. "Later."

~~~

Lucas looked into Mrs. Dutton's face. "She's asleep all right."

"She's kind of old so she probably needs to sleep." Colton commented. "Can we go downstairs and play with the cars?"

Lucas again looked into Mrs. Dutton's face and nodded his head yes. "Let's leave the TV on, if we turn it off, we might wake her up."

The three kids scrambled downstairs to what Sandy was now calling 'Dodge City.' She flipped on all the lights and everything lit up. The stop sign which was Colton's favorite, that was next to his green car, blinked red and green.

They spent the next hour racing around the streets of Dodge City. Sandy loved that old Western, Gunsmoke, and decided to name the town after Matt Dillon's, Dodge City. When she told her daddy he laughed and told her that he thought it was a great name. They had christened it with cokes and a pizza.
~~~

Colton asked Sandy about Dodge City. "Dodge City didn't have cars, only horses, and some chickens, but we haven't any horses and I haven't seen one chicken."

"Okay, Colton, listen to me. The right side where the Marshall's office is will be our Western side where Matt Dillon lives. That's Dodge City."

"Does Chester, Doc, and Kitty live there too?"

"Yes, they do. Now, the other side of the basement where our cars and the racetrack are is present day Dodge City, so we actually have two of them. One old, one new."

Colton thought for a minute and then said "okay, but we still don't have chickens."

Sandy would give Colton two plastic chickens in bright colors of red and yellow for Christmas that year. He proudly took them and placed them in Dodge City in front of the Marshall's office next to the hitching rail.

Lucas ran upstairs several times to check on Mrs. Dutton. He came down and sat next to Sandy. They were sitting in the chairs next to the Marshall's office.

He grinned at her, "who's babysitting who?"

"I guess she's just really tired tonight."

Lucas pointed over to Colton. He was sitting in his green car, which he had dubbed 'the magnificent green machine.' He was falling asleep. "we're going to have to take the green machine over to Dodge South." They had decided to call the modern Dodge, Dodge South so they would know which one they were talking about.

Sandy looked over at her brother and said, "let's put him to bed before he falls right out of the car."

Sandy went over and shook her brother. She leaned down to him and said "you need to go to bed."

He shook his head. "What about my magnificent green machine?"

"Lucas and I will put it away. It will be fine until the next time you need it."

Sandy and Lucas managed to get Colton undressed and into bed. He was so tired that he just rolled over and went back to sleep. They went downstairs to the TV room and sat down to watch another movie. The sound on the television drowned out the slight noise of a window sliding open. A figure dressed all in black crept in and went directly to the stairs, opened the door at the end of the hall and silently crept up to the attic. The Black figure turned on a flashlight, looked around, and then waited.

Jackson and Sarah had a wonderful time and were home by midnight. Jackson thanked Mrs. Dutton and walked her to her car.

"Will you be all right going home alone?"

"I've been taking myself home all my life. You go back your new to little sweetheart."

He chuckled and watched while she drove down the driveway and turn to the right. She didn't have that far to go, but he knew that when she got home, she would call him as she always did. It was their agreement.

Sarah looked at all the boxes around her. "Lucas and I will be back tomorrow and will get a handle on this."

"Don't make it too early. How about noon. We can grill some burgers for lunch."

"Noon it is."

Jackson walked Sarah and Lucas to the car. Lucas crawled into the back seat where he had a blanket and pillow. He was incredibly tired and curled up with the blanket.

"He needs his eight hours." Sarah laughed.

Jackson enveloped Sarah into his embrace and gently kissed her. "I had a great time."

"Me too."

"Call me when you get home."

"We'll be fine."

"Call anyhow."

Chapter 10

Sandy woke briefly. Something had been disturbing her, but she didn't know what it was. She sat up and listened to the quiet. She reflected how quiet had a sound of its own. The absence of sound around her was almost deafening in its own way. The quiet in the room was unnerving and it brought with it the reality that the silence was filling her with a creepy feeling of terror. She thought that nothing was truly blank, she heard nothing.

Sandy struggled as she tried to shake the empty feeling circling her. She looked around one last time and shrugged, she flipped her pillow several times, dug down under the covers and brought them up to her chin. She sighed deeply; she was letting her imagination run with her. She turned her thoughts to Lucas. She really liked him, he had been the first person she met when she came to Lone Mountain, they had become friends instantly. He was funny and made her laugh, he also was very tolerant of Colton, and even better, he was kind to him. She was really glad that he had found her that day.

Sandy's thoughts left her when she heard an unfamiliar sound. The house's deafening silence was now gone. They hadn't lived long in this house and it was fairly new to her, but she had already gotten familiar with its strangeness. Every night about 2 AM there was a swooshing sound that seemed to run throughout the entire house. It had woken her several times, but after a few days she barely acknowledged it. It was nothing more than a house noise. All houses had them. There was a clunk here, and a bang there, they were nothing to get excited about. It was just all part of what a house was.

The noise she just heard was not a known house noise. She sat motionless waiting for it to happen again and wasn't disappointed, two minutes later the scraping sound was followed by a slight knocking. It sounded like it came from above her bed. She froze. Her eyes went up to the ceiling above her, and then she waited again. A small scratching sound was accompanied by a long, low, high-pitched creak that sounded like a screeching as it drifted towards her. She felt goosebumps flowing up and down her body as she shook with fear.

There was a thump, a very dull sound against her half-closed bedroom door. Sandy squinted into the darkened room. There was no moon tonight, so the darkness that surrounded her was almost total. She could feel her heart pounding as she scooted down deeper into her covers. She stared into the gray black shadows hoping that nothing was going to leap out at her. Sandy continued to scan into the blackness of the room, her eyes darting from one spot to the other, she was looking for any type of movement. Her breathing had become shallow in an effort to remain quiet and unseen.

Sandy knew that she wasn't alone and that something else was present in the room, she could feel the danger flowing throughout the room. It was something evil.

From the doorway a series of wavy ridges seemed to move into a strange form, something that was flowing towards her. It moved and swayed and admitted a low growling sound. The figure seemed to blink in and out as it hissed to show its disapproval. It raised its arms in a threatening way and now she could actually feel the evil coming towards her. She knew that she was in danger. It looked pale against the darkness, like a ghost, the soul of the dead, and she knew it was after her. Sandy let out a piercing scream.

Black figure quickly left the bedroom and went downstairs to the window it had entered in. As quietly as possible it slipped back through the window and ran down the block disappearing into the darkness of the night.

~~~

Jackson bolted out of bed when he heard Sandy scream. She also woke Colton who cautiously moved to the doorway of his bedroom and peeked out into the hall. He saw his daddy hurrying over to Sandy's bedroom. She was still screaming.

Sandy was standing in the middle of the room with her eyes closed. Jackson immediately went to her and drew her into his arms. She was shaking uncontrollably. He took her over to the bed and sat down with her. He clicked on her bedside lamp which gave off a soft glow in the room. Sandy buried her face in her father's shirt and let out a deep sob. He pulled her closer and held her. Colton was standing in the doorway clutching his teddy bear, Norman, a tear rolled down his cheek.

Jackson looked over at his son and said, "come over here, son, there's nothing to be afraid of. Colton scurried over and jumped up on the bed next to his father, he moved as close as he possibly could and leaned against him. Jackson sat and held his children for several minutes before he turned Sandy's face up to look at him. "Sandy?"

It was horrible, daddy. It wanted to get me."

"There's no one here, but me and Colton."

"And Norman." Colton said holding up his black and white teddy bear.

Sandy laughed through her tears. "Stupid bear."

"He's not stupid." Colton said as he pulled Norman to his chest. "He's just used up some."

"Can you tell me what happened?" Jackson asked quietly.
~~~

"There was something in here with me. I heard it. I saw it. I could feel it."

"What exactly did you see?"

"It was kinda dark, but whatever it was seemed to show up in a murky gray color. It moved towards me and growled."

"Growled? Was it an animal?"

"No, it was a person. Somebody I couldn't see really clear." Sandy whispered. "It wanted to hurt me."

Jackson looked into her face, wiped her tears and said, "I'm going to look around. You, and Colton stay right here."

"Don't go, daddy."

"Do y'all want to come with me?"

"I don't think so."

Jackson kissed Sandy on the forehead. "I'll be right back."

Jackson walked through the entire house; he even went downstairs to Dodge city to make sure no one was there. After he was satisfied, he went back upstairs and sat down on the bed next to Sandy and Colton.

"There is no one in the house, but us."

"Did you look at all the bedrooms?"

"I did."

"Did you look in the bathrooms?"

"I looked in the bathrooms"

Sandy let her eyes roll up to the ceiling. "What about up there? What about the attic?"

"We haven't even been up to the attic. There's only one way up there and that's the doorway at the end of the hall. If someone had come through here, we would've seen them. I looked everywhere, even went down to Dodge City. Maybe you just had a bad dream"

"Yeah, bad dream." Echoed Colton.

"Can I sleep with you tonight, daddy?"

"I think that would be a good idea."

"Me, and Norman don't want to be alone. Can we come to?"

"Okay, but Norman better stay on his side of the bed."

Colton gave Jackson a somber look. "He will."

Chapter 11

When Sarah and Lucas arrived the next morning Jackson, Sandy, and Colton were still asleep. Colton pushed at his father, "Twilight Zones ringing."

Jackson rolled over and looked at the clock, it was after 12, he groaned. "Colton, run on down and let Sarah and Lucas in. Tell her we'll be down soon."

"Okay." Colton bolted off of the bed and hit the stairs at a full run.

Jackson poked Sandy. She opened her eyes and smiled up at him. "Are you, okay?"

"I guess so. Thanks for letting me sleep with you."

"Anytime you scared, or just need to be close, you know you can come to me."

"I will."

"You best get up get dressed, you don't want Lucas to catch you in your pajamas."

Jackson grabbed his jeans and his comfortable old green shirt that had definitely seen better days. It was almost threadbare.

Daddy, no." Sandy said from the doorway. That shirt should be thrown out. One wrong move and it'll fall apart. It looks terrible."

"Really?" He turned and looked in the mirror. "You're right."

Sandy held up the new yellow T-shirt that Colton had given him for his birthday. He took the other one and tossed it on the bed as he slipped into the yellow one.

"Much better. Honestly, daddy, who taught you how to dress?"

"I can hardly wait until you're a teenager." He laughed and hugged Sandy before sitting her down on the bed next to him. "Are you sure you're, okay?"

"I guess maybe it was just a dream like you said, but it really scared me and seemed so real."

"I will never let anything hurt you. The only explanation I can come up with is a bad dream. Let's forget it for now, we've got boxes to tackle. We have to get this house livable."

Jackson gave Sandy a quick kiss on the cheek and asked, "are you hungry?"

He went downstairs and asked the same question, all three kids yelled they were about ready to starve to death. He grinned, "everyone out on the deck. Cheeseburgers around."

Sarah grilled the burgers while Jackson organized the plates. Sandy helped her father and giggled. "It sure is a lot safer to eat around here now that Sarah is doing the cooking."

He swatted her playfully with the towel he had in his hand. "Nice thing to say about your daddy."

"Sarah doesn't burn everything."

"Well, hello, there everyone." Came a sing song voice from the side of the deck.

Sandy turned and found herself face to face with Lisa. She almost groaned out loud. "What are you doing here?"

When Colton saw Lisa, he buried his head in the teddy bear's belly. He didn't want to even look at her.

Jackson shot a look at Sandy and then turned to Lisa, "I didn't know you were coming?"

"I tried to call, Jackson, but no one answers the phone around here."

Lisa was only 5 feet two in her stocking feet. Her long brown hair hung down to her waist. Her blue eyes flashed at him, she looked like she was dressed for an Atlanta holiday. Her blue silk outfit showed off her shapely body. She reeked of sexuality. That was just the image she wanted to project.

Lisa giggled inside, next to Sarah she looked like a queen. Sarah was dressed in an old worn pair of jeans and a faded red shirt that looked like its freshness had been long gone. To her she looked like a rag picker.

"Sarah, I didn't know you would be here. I wanted to surprise Jackson and the children with a trip to Atlanta. There's a new play I thought the children would love." She drew out the word love.

"You should have called, Lisa, and I would've told you that I was unpacking today." Jackson gestured to the boxes. "I'm tired of walking around them and Sarah graciously offered to help."

Lucas and Sandy were sitting on the side of the deck. Lucas pointed to Lisa, "what's with her?"

"She's a pain. I don't like her at all. She's always trying to worm her way in. She's always getting touchy-feely with daddy. She hangs on him all the time and she comes over without ever calling, she just shows up and always tries to make me like her.

Sandy pitched her voice high. "Oh, Savanna, what a pretty dress you have on. Is that a new hairstyle? We must get together and go to Henri so he can make your style just perfect." She looked at Lucas. "All I do is comb it."

"Does your daddy know that you don't like her?"

"He knows all right, but he keeps saying she was momma's best friend and we have to be kind to her. I don't think he likes her either."

"You're welcome to stay for lunch, Lisa." Jackson offered. "We were just going to sit down."

"You bet your ass," Lisa thought. She wasn't going to leave Jackson along with this Bitch. She smiled and said, "I'd love to and I'll help y'all with the boxes."

Jackson didn't want Lisa to stay or to help unpacking, but she insisted she would. Right now, she was directing the children while sitting comfortably on the couch. Sandy rolled her eyes and said she was going to get some soda for everyone.

Lisa call to her, "Honey, I don't drink soda, could you get me a cup of tea?"

Sandy grumbled all the way into the kitchen. She pulled out six bottles of soda and one bottle of water. "Let her drink water. I'm not making her tea, or anything else."

She slammed the water down onto the tray. She thought she would throw up when she saw Lisa draping herself across her father.

"Need some help?"

Sandy looked over at Sarah. "She makes me so mad."

Sarah went over to the table and took the bottle of water off the tray; Sandy had slammed it down so hard it was leaking. She held up the bottle, "I can see that."

"The way she falls all over daddy. She's trying to worm her way into this family."

"Are you sure?"

"Yes, when momma died, she was right there trying to take her place. I don't like her, and I know for sure she doesn't like me. She's a real phony." Sandy turned to Sarah and with insight way beyond her years she said, "she wants daddy because he's got a lot of money. She doesn't want me, or Colton."

"Are you sure? You may just feel that way because you don't like her."

"Ask Colton. When daddy isn't looking, she pushes him. I saw her do it and I told daddy, but Lisa said it was an accident, she said that she slipped."

Sarah sat down at the table and patted the chair across from her. She took Sandy's hand in hers and smiled. "I know you don't like Lisa; it might be best if you try to talk to your father about this again."

"I know, but all daddy will say is she's was momma's best friend and she's hurting too. I wish she would go away and never come back here."

"I understand, but as long as you daddy wants her to visit, I'm afraid you'll have to be nice to her." As an afterthought Sarah said, "give her the water."

They spent the rest of the day unpacking boxes with Lisa remaining on the couch directing. Jackson decided everyone had had enough. "It's time to quit for today. Everyone did a great job and it's time to order pizza."

"Oh, Jackson, sweetie, just a big old salad for me. Pizza can be so fattening. Don't you agree, Sarah?"

"I think pizza sounds definitely wonderful."

Jackson winked at her. "The purest kind?"

"Is there any other way?"

Lisa was furious. Now they had some kind of private joke going. This wasn't good, wasn't good at all and it wasn't acceptable. She had to break this up. She would think on the problem.

Jackson looked around and realize that Colton wasn't there. "Where's Colton?"

"He was here a little while ago, daddy."

"Colton." Jackson called. "Colton. Everyone spread out and look for him."

"Wait, daddy. Try Dodge City."

Lisa looked strangely at Sandy, "what's Dodge City?"

Jackson found Colton down in Dodge City. He had gone into the Marshall's office and crawled onto a cot in one of the jail cells and fell asleep. Jackson leaned down and shook him. He looked up.

"What are you doing down here all alone?"

"I was tired and wanted to be alone."

"I understand. Are you hungry? I ordered pizza."

"Is it all right if I eat it later?"

"Sure, but you have to go nap in your bed not down here, it's too cold."

"I could get a blanket."

"No. Come on."

Colton held up his arms, "carry me."

Jackson carried Colton up to his bedroom. "Take off your jeans and you'll sleep easier."

Colton struggled with his pants, but was having no success at all. "Daddy, their stuck."

Jackson had opened the dresser to get a T-shirt for Colton and turned to see his son standing with his pants pooled around his ankles. "You're supposed to take off your shoes and socks first."

He looked down at his shoes and said, "I forgot."

Jackson pulled off his tennis shoes and took off his socks before slipping the jeans off. Colton shook his head, "that works better."

Jackson covered Colton and felt his forehead. He was worried that maybe he didn't feel well, it wasn't like him to take naps anymore. "Come down when you're ready."

Colton pulled Norman over to him and hugged him close to his chest. "When is Lisa going away?"

"Is that the problem?"

Colton shrugged. "She'll be leaving pretty soon, after we finish with the pizza."

"Okay." Colton rolled over and hugged the teddy bear even tighter.

As Jackson walked down the stairs he thought about Lisa. The kids definitely didn't like her around. Sandy said she was trying to take her momma's place, but Colton said she was mean to him. He didn't know what to think.

The doorbell rang its Twilight Zone, Sandy went to open it. "Daddy. Pizza."

They sat down on the deck. He watched as Lisa wiped the chair before she would even sit in it. Sarah turned all her attention to Jackson, "is Colton alright?"

"I think we just wore him out, sometimes I forget he's just a little guy."

Once they were all seated Jackson noticed that Lucas was favoring his left hand. He had some type of bandage on it that was bloodied. "Lucas, what did you do to your hand?"

Lucas looked down at the bloodied handkerchief he had wrapped around his hand. "I cut it with a knife when I was opening one of the boxes."

Lisa gagged at the sight of blood. "Oh..... My..... God....."

"It's not too bad, it's just bleeding some."

Jackson went over and sat down next to Lucas. He gestured to his hand. "Let's have a look."

He unwrapped the makeshift bandage and looked up at Lucas. "This looks like it needs to be stitched. You should've told me that you got hurt."

"I didn't think it was all that bad."

Sarah looked at her son's hand and shook her head in agreement, "it looks deep."

Lucas flexed his hand and more blood appeared. "Guess y'all are right, it does hurt some."

"Lisa turned her head away and said, "I think I'll faint."

"Don't." Jackson said. "One patient is enough." He turned back to Lucas, how bad does it hurt?"

"Kinda bad."

"I'll bet. Let me go and get my bag. Come with me to the kitchen."

Sandy got up from her chair. "Can I watch?"

"Sure, I always appreciate a consultation."

Sarah went over to Jackson and whispered, "I better stay here just in case Lisa does decide to faint."

"We won't be long."

When Jackson left with the children Lisa turned to Sarah. "Jackson and I are very close; we have been for many years. Mary, his wife and I were the best of friends. Before she died," Lisa lied. "I promised her I would take care of Jackson."

Sarah answered her in a toneless voice. "I thought she was murdered?"

"What I meant was that we had talked like years ago and agreed if either one of us died unexpectedly the other would take care of things."

"Is Jackson one of those things?"

Lisa gave her a cold stare. "Yes, he is." As an afterthought she added, "and her children, of course."

Of course." Sarah agreed.

"The point is that I am here to do just that, and I am here to stay."

"And what do Jackson and the children want? I think he's more than capable of taking care of himself and his children."

Jackson took his doctor's bag down from the shelf and searched for suture material. He had Lucas soaking his hand with Sandy closely supervising. When he found what he was looking for he went over to the table and sat directly next to Lucas. He laid everything out on a sterile pad, turned and smiled at the boy.

"Okay, I'm going to give you a local anesthetic so that I can close this up."

"How many stitches, daddy?"

"Maybe five."

Jackson carefully sutured the wound close, he put in exactly 5 stitches.

Sandy looked on approvingly, "good job, daddy."

"Thank you. Now, comes the hard part."

"What's that, Doc?"

Jackson held up a syringe. "Tetanus shot."

"That's so you don't lock up your jaws and go foaming at the mouth." Sandy advised him."

Jackson gave her a look, "Sandy."

"It can happen, daddy."

Jackson gave Lucas the injection and bandaged his hand. "You'll be fine and we'll take the stitches out in about seven days."

"Thanks, Doc."

Sarah and Lucas left around 8 PM. Lisa stayed. Jackson was tired and wanted nothing more than to go to bed.

He turned to Lisa, "it's getting late, and I am really ready to crash."

"I'm sorry today didn't work out for us. How about tomorrow? We could still go to Atlanta; the kids would love to go to the show and then you and I can have some alone time."

"Lisa had moved closer to Jackson and then threw her arms around his neck. "I would love to have some alone time with you."

Sandy was on the staircase going up to her room when she heard Lisa in the entranceway. She watched as Lisa moved against her father, she rolled her eyes, "ICK." She was going to put a stop to this. "Daddy."

She went down the stairs and into the entranceway. "Oh, Lisa, I thought you had left. Sorry."

Lisa moved slightly away from Jackson and glared at Sandy. Sandy went over to her father. "I'm not feeling very well. My stomach is really achy and I think maybe I'm going to throw up."

He lightly placed his hand on her forehead. "Go to your bedroom, sweetheart, and I'll be up in a minute."

"All right." Sandy moved slowly to the stairs, looked back and then started up even slower.

"I think tomorrow is out. Sandy doesn't feel well and I still have a lot of work to do around here. Another time."

"Well, I'm staying at my aunts until tomorrow night. If Sandy feels better, call me."

Jackson held the door open for her. He took a step backwards and said, "good night, Lisa."

She took two steps forward and kissed his cheek. "Good night, sweetie."

"Be careful. The roads can be dark this time of night."

Jackson went upstairs to Sandy's bedroom and walked over to her bed, he looked down at her. "You aren't really sick, are you?"

"No, not really. Lisa kinda makes me sick if that counts."

Jackson shrugged, "no, it doesn't."

"I don't like her. She's always hanging on you and trying to insert herself into our lives. Daddy, there's something about her, something not right, I can feel it. Is she coming over here tomorrow?"

"No. I told her we had a lot to do yet, and I have to go back to work on Monday."

"Good." Sandy thought it was good idea to change the subject. "How's the lady with the baby?

"The baby is doing well, but his momma has a long road to recovery."

"Will she get well?"

"I don't know. She's very sick right now."

"I'm sorry, I don't like Lisa. I tried, I really did, but I can't warm up to her."

"I think I understand. Crawl under those covers and go to sleep, don't worry about it."

Sandy wrapped her arms around her father and kissed him. "Thanks, daddy, I love you."

"Love you right back. Sleep tight."

Jackson went to his bedroom and thought about Lisa. He wasn't sure that he actually liked her either. He had always welcome her into his home because of his wife, and their friendship. Sandy was right, Lisa seemed to be pushing herself into their life's and he didn't want that. She had become demonstrative, hanging all over him and being overly affectionate in front of Sarah. This was something he definitely didn't want. He had no intentions of any type of romantic interest and had gently tried to tell her.

He decided right there that he was going to limit communication and any direct contact with her whenever possible.

Chapter 12

Paul looked over at his brother. They were in the crappy apartment they had rented and it was a mess. Old boxes of carry out food sat everywhere. Alvin was eating a piece of cold pizza and drinking a flat beer. They were almost out of money.

Alvin threw down the pizza, got up, and went over to the television to turn it off. He sat down on the footstool across from his brother. "Why can't we get the money and split?"

"I told you, it's too soon. We can't afford to be picked up with all of that jewelry on us."

"We could fence it."

"And that would lead the cops right to our door."

"If we don't get some money, we aren't going to have a place to stay, let alone a door."

"We can always do a Stop and Rob."

"Why don't we get out of this town."

"Because I want to be close to the money. Until this cools down, we have to stay put. Right now, it's all over the papers and television. That detective, Lenny, something isn't dumb."

"It can't be traced to us. We didn't leave anything behind."

"What do you call our dead former partner, Stanley Richards? And what about Mandy?"

"Mandy is still alive. Well, barely still alive."

"And what about my kid?"

"He's in what they call a baby intensive care."

"It's a boy?"

"Yeah, it was a boy. Guess he's not doing so good either."

"I want you to go back to the hospital Alvin, and find out exactly how bad the baby is. I want the kid, also we need to know if Mandy is going to recover."

"Do you expect me to just walk out of the hospital with a sick baby?"

"That's exactly what I expect you to do."

"Why? I thought you didn't care."

"He's mine and if Mandy survives it's a way to control her."

"Okay, I'll go snoop around today. I'm going to wait until three because it's busiest around shift change.

"Later we'll do the convenience store and get some money. The end of the day should work before they bank the money."

"If I snatch the kid, what do we do with it while we go to work?"

"He can stay here."

"Alone?"

"Sure, why not?"

"Because it's only a few days old and a sick kid."

"Just go over there and get it done."

Alvin pulled his coat on and went out to his car. He hoped it was still working because he didn't have time to go and steal another one. He tried to start it, but it sputtered and died. He slammed his hand against the steering wheel in frustration.

Alvin sat for a moment, took a deep breath, and tried again. He was surprised and relieved when the engine caught. He made sure that he drove safely and obeyed all of the traffic rules. Once he got to the hospital, he pulled into the fourth floor of the parking lot. He didn't hurry, he walked through the emergency room entrance as if he didn't have a care in the world.

Sarah looked up from behind the window in the emergency room, but the man didn't stop, he kept walking. Something about the man disturbed her, but she forgot him immediately when an ambulance with lights and sirens rolled up. She called to the nurse behind her, "page Dr. Shepard."

The ambulance arrived with a 55-year-old woman, Alice States, she had been shot seven times and was clinging to life. Alice and her boyfriend, Red Patrick, lived in the Pierce Akers Development together. Pierce Akers was low-income housing that was noted for violence. It was 10 miles outside of Lone Mountain. The Sheriff's Department was out there on an almost daily basis.

Red and Alice had gotten into an argument over who was paying for their take-out pizza. It started quietly, but became violent within minutes when neither would give in. Alice hit Red over the head with a lamp. He had a deep gash that was bleeding profusely. Red ran to the bathroom, grabbed the only towel in there and held it to his head. When he got the bleeding under control, he went to the bedroom and got his Smith & Wesson 22 from the drawer, then he went back to Alice.

Red never said a word, he just started shooting. When he was done, he patiently waited for the pizza delivery. Alice was lying on the doorstep when the man came to deliver the pizza. Red looked down at her and said, "she's sleeping." He held out a $20 bill to the driver. The driver took the money, went back to his car and called the Sheriff's Department.

Alvin walked over to the ICU and talk to the nurse, Marybelle Hunt. "I just found out about my friend, Mandy, is there a possibility that I could talk to her?"

"I'm sorry, she's unconscious and has been ever since she was admitted. She will not be able to respond in any way."

"Can you tell me about her condition? Will she regain consciousness?"

"You would have to speak to her doctor."

"Who is that?"

"Dr. Jackson Shepard. He should be in the hospital, if you go downstairs the reception can page him for you."

Alvin thanked the nurse and left. The entire encounter with her took less than three minutes, he made it as short as possible because he didn't want anyone to have enough time to identify him. He went down to reception because he wanted to check where the baby was. He quickly discovered that he was on a locked unit.

"Great."

Alvin sat down, picked up a magazine and waited. It wasn't long before two ladies, their arms filled with gifts went to the door. He got up and walked behind them. They were admitted into the ward. He followed them down to the end of the hall where the two women entered room 227. He quickly went to the left, he wondered exactly where this pediatric care unit was at. He saw several nurses, but they were all sitting at the nurse's station and seem to be involved in some kind of paperwork.

"Can I help you, sir?"

Alvin turned around, *where the hell did she come from?* He smiled, it was a kid, probably some kind of volunteer. A snotty little 14 or 15-year-old kid.

"Yes, ma'am, I'm looking for my nephew, he's in the pediatric intensive care."

"You're in the wrong place. Pediatric intensive care is down on the second floor. East wing."

"Thank you."

Alvin was spooked and went directly to the exit. "Screw this."

After he left the floor, he made a fast retreat out of the hospital. He wasn't going to chance getting arrested.

"Where's the kid?" Paul screamed.

"I told you, I couldn't even get close to him. They keep them bottled up in a special ward, under lock and key."

Paul had been pacing, "What did you find out about Mandy?"

"The bitch is in some kind of coma. We're okay as long as she can't talk."

"Okay. Here's what we're going to do. First, we have to get some money, so tonight we go out and take care of that, then were going to take care of Mandy so she can never point a finger at either of us."

Chapter 13

Jackson had a hard day. He worked for over three hours trying to save Alice States life, but she had a heart attack during the procedure and couldn't survive it. He felt it was due to all of the blood loss. He felt she wouldn't survived when he had first seen her come into the emergency room.

Jackson worked the emergency room twice a week, he enjoyed the challenge of it. He encountered many things that he wouldn't see in private practice. He also felt it kept his medical skills sharp, and there was a plus to it, he got to see Sarah. When things were quiet, they could enjoy being together. Before he left for the day, they had agreed to have dinner together tomorrow.

He asked her with the slightest smile, "kids, or no kids?"

"Kids. I'll bring the burgers."

~~~

Sarah kicked off her shoes and stretched. Jackson grinned at her bright orange toenails. She grinned back at him, "what?"

He pointed to her toes. "They're cute."

"Where are the kids?"

"Down in Dodge, there plotting their next adventure."

"I'm so happy that they get along so well."

Jackson sat down on the lounge chair next to her. He leaned down and kissed her. "I'm glad that we all get along."
~~~

From the side of the deck he heard, "daddy." Sandy stepped onto the deck. "Guess who's here?"

He took a deep breath. "Lisa?"

"It is Friday and she has a habit of showing up on Fridays."

"Where is she?"

"I stashed her in the family room. Do you want me to tell her to go away?"

"No, you go back down to Dodge and I'll speak with Lisa.

Lisa had actually followed Sandy to the deck and now she ran over to Jackson, threw her arms around him, and kissed him on the mouth.

Jackson quickly disengaged her grip and stepped back. "What are you doing here, Lisa? I thought we agreed you would call first."

"I was in the area and I wanted to see you. I didn't think you would mind."

Sarah didn't say a word, she got up and walked by them and went into the house. She decided it was time for her to go to Dodge.

Sandy met her at the steps. "What's going on?"

"Your father is having a discussion with Lisa. I thought they could talk easier if I wasn't there."

"I wish she would go away and not come back here."

Jackson went down the stairs and called out. Sandy yelled from the other into the room, "we're down here, daddy, at the end."

He strolled through Dodge and over to the post office where Sarah stood smiling broadly at him. "Hey, big boy, do you come here often?"

"Sure do, ma'am. Every chance I get."

"Where's your shadow?"

"I sent her home. We've talked about this before, and I told her again that she can't just show up anytime she wants to."

"Did she have your weekend planned for you?"

"She sure did, but I'm spending the weekend, well, Sunday anyhow, with you. I have to work on Saturday. I promised Dr. Cary Long, I'd work the emergency room shift for him."

"That's perfect, drop Sandy and Colton over to my place and I'll have dinner ready for you when you're done with your shift."

"Woman, you're in my heart. You are perfect, right down to your bright orange toenails, a man couldn't ask more than to have dinner waiting for him when he came home."

After watching the movie with the children, Jackson turned to Sarah and asked, "can you tell me more about this house? Sandy seems to think it's haunted."

"That actually is the rumor around here. It goes back many, many years."

"Do you want to share?"

"Sure."

"Wait." Lucas said. "I want to get Sandy and Colton because they'll want to hear this." Lucas came back with Sandy and Colton, she handed her father a soda, and then one for Sarah. The three children sat down to listen to the story.

"As you already know, the original people who lived here were the Lansing's. They are very secretive and never participated in any town events. I've lived here all of my life, born and raised, and I remember them, vaguely. I do remember what happened.

It was late September when it all started, it seemed that several people here in Lone Mountain, and over to Marrow had been reported missing. Not one of them was found over a six-month period, not until September.

Mr. Alvin Lansing reported that his wife, Alice Jean, and their daughter, Amanda also went missing. He said they went to Atlanta for a day of shopping and never came home. Jackson, are you sure you want the children to hear all of this?"

Jackson looked over at Sandy and Colton. Colton was lying on the floor fast asleep. Sandy looked at her brother and then back at her father. "Daddy, I'm not a little child."

"But you are a child, something you seem to forget."

"I've heard it all before, Doc. It's not that awful."

"Go ahead, Sarah, let's hear the rest."

"Mrs. Lansing was found at Four Crossing Road halfway between Atlanta and here. Someone had cut her throat and placed her body next to the five other bodies that were missing. They were all dead. They were lying in a meadow of alfalfa, 12 miles north of Lone Mountain. All the bodies were surrounded by trees, bushes, and a smattering of herbs. Bright yellow flowers that look like Buttercup surrounded all of the bodies. The area was so silent it casted an eeriness to it. It was kind of spooky and as strange as it was, it was frightening. No one ever found the killer, or why Alice Jean Lansing was placed with the other victims. She had been killed sometime later than the rest of the victims. This answered the question of whether she was missing or dead. None of the murders were solved.

Two days after they found Alice Jean, they found Bobby Joe Lansing, he had been dead for several weeks. Four days after that, the father, Alvin Lansing hung himself in this house."

Sandy gasped and grabbed Lucas's hand. She pointed to the upstairs. "Up there?"

"Off of the banister."

"It means nothing, Sandy." Jackson said to reassure his daughter. "I think that's enough discovery for tonight."

"We need to know the rest, daddy, it doesn't scare me."

"There's not too much more. The daughter, Amanda was never found. Some think that she's also dead, but others say, she just wanted to disappear and is still out there somewhere."

"What do you think, momma?"

"I'd like to think that she somewhere having a happy life, and that is enough for tonight besides we don't know if all this is true."

"Jackson touched her hand. "Is there more?"

"Just a little, but I'll tell you later."

"Wait when?"

"When were both working tomorrow."

~ ~ ~

Jackson walked into the emergency room and immediately looked for Sarah. He wanted to finish the conversation from last night. This curiosity was killing him. What she had told him was horrible, he had talked to Sandy about it, but she said it didn't bother her.

"How many kids can say they live in a house where someone hung themselves."

Jackson found Sarah in the last room on the left. "Sarah."

"Hey, Jackson."

"Do we have any patients?"

"So far, it's been very quiet."

"Good." He took her hand and led her over to the coffee room directly across from the emergency. He poured them each a cup of coffee, handed one to Sarah and sat down next to her.

"What?"

"Finish the story from last night. What didn't you tell me?"

"I thought the hanging thing was more than enough for the kids to digest."

"I spoke with Sandy and she's not having a problem with it. Colton was asleep, so he knows nothing. I want to try to do rounds so let's finish this."

"Okay, your house is haunted."

Jackson was startled by what she said. "Haunted?" He stammered.

"Yes, haunted."

"Who's haunting it?"

"Well, the theory is................... "

"Wait." He said putting up his hand. "Who exactly said that it's haunted?"

"The Crawford family. They rented the house, but only stayed for six days, it took them that long to run. Mr. Crawford said they couldn't stay in the house that made so much noise."

"What noise?"

"Just noise."

"Did anyone else hear the noise besides him?"

"Yes. According to Brenda Crawford, that was his wife, she said she heard moaning, rattling chains, and the constant ringing coming from places unknown. The husband, Brent, claims that he saw an older woman who he thinks is Mrs. Alice Jean Lansing. He was sitting in the family room and claimed Alice Jean just drifted in and walked around calling for her husband.

Jackson, I don't believe what the Crawford's claimed. Have you had any trouble with banging or ghosts floating around?"

"Why did the Crawford's bolt after six days?"

The question was never answered because two ambulances came roaring up to the emergency room ramp, interrupting the story once again.

Jackson finished with the emergency room at 6 o'clock that evening and then went to see his patients. He walked into the intensive care unit and over to Mandy's bed.

"She seems to be a little better." Nurse Jo Marie Coffee said from behind him. "She's had some eye flutter and movement. Seems like her level of consciousness has lightened."

Jackson examined Mandy and agreed she seemed to be improving. He ordered a scan of her brain for tomorrow. He leaned down and squeezed her hand, "hang in there, kid."

Jackson left the intensive care unit and walked down to the pediatric intensive care. He went in, nodded to the night nurse, Carol Lee. "Where is baby Sterling?"

"Oh, you mean little Jackson. He's in bed 108."

"Jackson?"

"We had to give him a name and since you brought the little guy into the world, we decided to call him Jackson.

He smiled broadly, "Thanks, Carol."

He went over to bed 108, and looked down at the little baby. He was born premature and was very small. "Hey, Jackson."

He carefully picked up the baby and cuddled him close. He sat down on one of the many rocking chairs in the unit and moved slowly back and forth. Carol walked over to Jackson and smiled.

"He's doing much better, at first, he had a little trouble taking the bottle." Carol held out a bottle of formula. "It's feeding time for this little guy."

Jackson took the bottle, leaned back and offered it to the baby. He took it eagerly. "That a boy. I knew you could do it. It's been a long time since I did this so let's go slow."

Chapter 14

Jackson, Sandy, and Colton finally finished unpacking all of the boxes. They no longer had to walk over them. "Finally." Sandy said, "I didn't think we'd ever get it done."

Colton pointed to the corner. "There's one more."

Sandy groaned. "I don't think I can do one more box."

"Relax, and I'll handle it."

Jackson opened the box and turned to his daughter. "This one is yours. I'll put it in your bedroom."

"Great. What could I possibly have forgotten?"

Jackson looked into the box again. "It's pink."

Sandy went over and also looked into the box, "my quilt. I kinda wondered what happened to it."

Colton peered into the box and then over at his father. "Can we go over to the Last Pizza Stop for dinner?"

"Sure, why not."

"Can we call Sarah and Lucas to come?"

"I think that would be a wonderful idea."

Jackson ordered three pizzas and then went back to the table. "Daddy, can we go play in the video arcade?"

Jackson pulled out his wallet and handed each child five dollars. Lucas looked at the money and then looked at his mother.

"It's okay, Lucas." Jackson reassured him. "Take the money and go have fun."

"Thanks, Doc."

After they left Sarah turned to him, "you shouldn't do that."

"Why? It's not a big thing."

"He's not supposed to take money from anyone."

"He's not taking money from anyone; he's taking it from his future father."

Sarah couldn't have been more surprised by the statement. "What exactly does that mean?"

"I am falling hopelessly in love with you, and I'm going to marry you."

"What do I say to that?"

"You could say that you love me. If not, how about you like me a lot."

"I do like you, more than like you, but your………"

Jackson took her hand. "Don't say anything right now. I'll continue to love you and you can continue to really like me until I convince you that you love me and can't live without me. After that we get married."

Sarah was saved from answering when the kids came back and the pizza arrived. Jackson grinned at her, a real cat grin, and then reached over to kiss her cheek. "To be continued." He whispered.

~~~

Jackson tucked the covers around Sandy. He leaned down and kissed her. "Did you have a good day?"
~~~

"It would be better if I didn't have to go to school tomorrow."

"Sorry, but tomorrow's Friday and you'll have the entire weekend to play with Lucas."

"Are you going to work this weekend?"

"No, I have the entire weekend off."

Sandy screwed up her face. "What about Lisa? Is she coming?"

"I told her we weren't available this weekend."

"Good."

"Sandy, how do you feel about Sarah?"

"She's really great, and a good hugger."

"She is that."

"You really like her, don't you daddy?"

"Very much."

"I like having her around. I miss momma, and she does a lot of things like she did. She's also really nice to Colton and never too busy to talk to us about anything. Oh, and she can cook without burning the food."

"Good night, sweetheart."

"Good night, daddy."

~ ~ ~

Lisa had followed Jackson, Sarah, and the children to the restaurant. She took a booth directly in the back where she could see them at an angle. She watched carefully and could feel the anger flooding into her. He laughed and touched her gently on the arm, he was hers and shouldn't be doing that. She had the sinking feeling that he was slowly slipping away from her, but that would change because she had a plan.

Lisa left before Jackson, Sarah, and the kids. She wanted to make sure that they didn't see her.

~~~

Sandy woke up and was confused. She thought she heard a loud thump from somewhere so she sat up in the bed and listen for what seemed a long time, nothing happened.

She shrugged and pulled the covers up and got herself comfortable once again. She was just about asleep when she heard something that frightened her. She jumped up when she heard footsteps running toward her.

A black figure crept into her bedroom. It seemed to slither slowly, hesitate, and start all over again. It moved smoothly and came closer towards her. At first the black figure seemed small, but the closer he got the larger it appeared.

Sandy felt her skin crawl as she watched it come even closer. She backed up into the corner by the headboard and froze. It continued forward, when it crossed the lit window where the moon shone brightly, it hesitated before shrinking back into the shadows.

She could feel anger and hostility admitting from it, it was directed at her. It reeked of something sinister and dark. Sandy closed her eyes and screamed.

The black figure retreated into the houses shadow and left. Jackson bolted out of bed and ran to Sandy's bedroom when he heard her scream. She was sitting in the middle of the bed, her hands tightly over her eyes, sobbing. He pulled her into his arms as she shook violently, she grabbed him.

"Easy, baby, easy. Everything's all right."
~~~

"No, it's not. It growled at me again. It hates me, it wants to eat me."

"Nothing's going to eat you. Look at me Sandy." He lifted her chin so that she was looking directly at him. "There is no one here, just us, me, you, and Colton."

"Where is Colton?" She hiccupped.

"Somehow he seemed to have slept through all this."

It took Jackson an hour to calm Sandy and convince her that she was having nothing more than a bad dream. He lay down in the bed next to her and held her until she fell asleep.

~~~

Jackson put hot biscuits on the table to go with their eggs. Sandy picked one up and turned it over in her hand. "It's burnt, daddy." She poked at the other biscuits, "they're all burnt."

He picked up a biscuit. "You're right."

"That's okay, you'll get it right one of these days."

They both laughed when Colton took a bite of his biscuit. He shrugged, "I'm getting kind of use to them."

"Now, that's just pathetic."

"Do you feel better this morning?"

"I think so. Daddy, why do I keep seeing monsters? It seemed so real."

"I don't know. Is there something bothering you?"

"Just school. I can't wait for to be over."

"It's only March." He said dryly. "You've a long way to go. Is there anything else that's bothering you?"
~~~

"Do we have a ghost in this house?"

"Not that I know of."

"How about in the attic?" Colton said.

"Attic. Daddy, we haven't even been up there. What if someone is living up there and that's who comes down at night to scare me."

"No one is living in the attic."

"You don't know that. There could be someone up there right now." Whispered Sandy.

Jackson got up, took a flashlight, and went to the stairs.

"Where's he going?" Asked Colton.

Sandy put down her fork, got up and followed her father. Colton took her hand and together they went to the doorway leading into the attic.

"Daddy, are you up there?" Sandy called from the bottom of the stairs.

"I'll be right down, Sandy."

Jackson came down from the attic and sat on the bottom step. "No ghosts. No live people, nothing but a lot of things the former owner, or owners must've left." He looked at the children, "Saturday we're going exploring because that attic is busting with things. I think we'll ask Sarah and Lucas to come and join us on the hunt."

Chapter 15

Jackson made a very important stop before he went home. He walked through the door and shouted, "where's my favorite kids."

Sandy and Colton ran from the family room, but stopped short when they saw what was wiggling in their father's arms.

"Where did you get him?"

"Him is a her." He held out the brown, black, and white puppy. I thought you could use a friend to sleep with you, maybe it will help you sleep better."

He handed the puppy to Sandy who hugged her close. Colton patted the dog's head. "She's beautiful. Thank you, daddy."

"What's her name?"

"Anything you would like to name her."

"Come on, Colton."

They took the puppy into the family room and sat on the floor with her. For the next hour they threw names back and forth at each other. Finally, they decided on the name; Stormy.

"Why Stormy?"

"Look at her, daddy, she has a bunch of colors mixed in like a summer storm."

Jackson picked up the puppy, her long tongue stretched to reach him. She had long hair that was mixed with black, brown, and white, he thought there was even a spattering of red. He smiled broadly and his children, "good name."

Jackson's cell phone rang, he answered it, "Dr. Shepard."

"That's very official."

"Sarah, good morning, sweetheart."

~~~

Sarah and Lucas arrived an hour later. She held up a package, "I brought dinner."

Colton took the steaks and put them into the refrigerator for later.

"We're going to tackle the attic, and prove to Sandy that there is nothing up there that she needs to be afraid of."

"Is she still having nightmares?"

"Two nights ago, she woke me up screaming again."

Sandy tore into the kitchen with Stormy close behind her. The dog stopped when she saw Sarah and Lucas. She backed up and growled at them, then let out a loud yip.

Sandy giggled. "It's okay Stormy, this is my friend Lucas in his momma, Sarah."

Lucas went down to his knees and called to the puppy. She cautiously approached him, sniffed, and yipped falling over backwards. The children took the dog outside to play with her.

Jackson took Sarah into his arms and held her tightly. He gave her a long, passionate kiss. "I've missed you."

"We saw each other yesterday."

He snorted, "ain't love grand?"

Jackson led everyone up the stairs and into the attic. He stepped aside so that they could see all of the things that seemed to be everywhere.
~~~

"Holy cow."

"I know. I had no idea all this was up here, Sarah. The first time I came up here was the night before last."

"How can anyone have this much stuff?"

"I haven't a clue, but I figure it will take a good month to go through all of this. I might even have to get a dumpster."

Sarah threw up her hands, "where do we start?"

"Let's start by making a bigger path through the middle here. Just kind of move things to the side, if you can."

The kids had already started crawling over furniture in their exploration. To them this was a big adventure into an unknown territory.

"Sandy." Colton yelled.

"Sandy, Lucas, come look, come on, hurry."

Colton had found a large, life-sized wooden horse in the corner of the room. He stood before the dark brown horse that had a flowing white mane and tail. On its back was a leather saddle that had been hand tooled, decorated in swirls of roses and stained even a darker brown than the horse. It was the most beautiful thing Colton had ever seen. He lightly touched the mane.

"I've got to have him. You think daddy will put him downstairs in my bedroom?"

"He's kind of big." Lucas said. "But it can't hurt to ask."

Jackson and Sarah stood in front of the wooden horse who now was being called Buck after Matt Dillons horse. He looked down at Colton who was eagerly waiting his decision.

"I'll need help to get him downstairs, but you can definitely have him, and if you want him in your bedroom, that's where he'll go."

"Soon, daddy?"

"As soon as I can."

They spent the afternoon going through most of the attic. Colton would often run back to Buck and gently pat his mane. Stormy got tired, found a stuffed chair and made herself comfortable. Sarah was astonished not only at the number of things cluttering the attic, but at the variety. The entire attic seemed to be filled from the front of the room to the back.

The narrow path that they attempted to make larger ran through the center of the room and was their only way around unless they climbed over something. The things in the attic went from pure junk, they had found a box of broken toys that looked like someone had purposely smashed them, to antique collectibles. There were also boxes of old fashion, out of date, broken pieces of something they couldn't identify.

"Jackson, what do we do now?"

"Okay, everybody listen up. Anything that you find broken, or obviously ugly bring it to the front. We'll start by getting rid of what no one wants to keep. In other words, we throw out the trash."

"Okay, daddy."

"Got it, Doc."

Everyone went back to work with renewed enthusiasm and they spent the next two hours examining and eliminating. When they were done there was a pool of junk sitting by the door. Jackson had brought up large reinforced garbage bags and an assortment of boxes to put the trash in.

He laughed when he saw the big note tied around the wooden horse's neck. Colton had written, "not junk. Don't throw out Buck."

They were all tired, but Sarah insisted on grilling. Jackson protested, saying that they could order out, but she wouldn't hear of it. Sandy looked at her father, "she wins. And letting her do the cooking is best for all of us."

~~~

Two days later disaster would strike. Jackson got a call from the hospital at 10 PM. He called Mrs. Dutton to come and watch the kids, and then left immediately for the hospital.

When he got to the hospital, Sarah was having a CAT scan. He went down to CAT scan and walked into the adjoining room. He could see only her feet sticking out from the machine.

"Dr. Belton, Jackson Shepard."

"Doctor, I guess you want to know about our Sarah."

"Yes."

While they were talking Jackson was looking at the head scan. "What do you see?" Dr. Belton asked,

"The scan seems to be normal except for right here." He pointed to a small dark area.

"Brain bleed. Very small. She definitely has a concussion, a broken left arm, and some lacerations on both legs. Dr. Sterling will cast her arm later. She's going to have some time in the hospital." Dr. Belton turned to Jackson. "She'll be fine barring any complications which I don't think will happen."

Jackson let out a sigh of relief that he didn't even know he had been holding.
~~~

"Her son," Dr. Belton continued. "Is fine except for some bruising and cuts from the window glass. He has stitches in his right arm."

"Where is Lucas?"

"I believe he's still in the emergency room. Go, she'll be going to room 118 and about 45 minutes."

"Thank you, doctor."

Jackson hurried upstairs to the emergency room. He found Lucas in Bay two. He was laying with his eyes closed, he went to his bedside and fell for a pulse. Lucas opened his eyes, "momma?"

Jackson bent down and said, "she has a concussion, and a broken arm. She's going to have to stay in the hospital for a while. Lucas, what happened?"

"I'm not sure. My head hurts so bad, everything happened so fast. The car started to swerve and momma couldn't get it straight. We were up on Tanner Hill, it was lucky we didn't go over, the side rail, it saved us. We hit the mountainside hard. The next thing I knew, I was here. I'm really scared."

Jackson took Lucas's hand in his. "You don't have to be afraid. Your momma will be fine and so will you."

Lucas attempted to get up, grabbed his head and started to moan. Jackson helped ease him back down into a prone position. "Easy, you have a bruise right here," he pointed to the black and blue that was starting below his eyes. "I'm going to give you something for your headache, but you have to stop moving around."

"Doc, I have nowhere to go. It's just me and momma and I can't go home alone."

"Stop worrying. You're going to come home with me, but first I want you to rest and as soon as your momma is in her room, we will go see her together."

Jackson not only wanted Lucas to see that Sarah was all right, he wanted that assurance for himself as well. He let Lucas rest for a couple hours and then went back for him. He buttoned Lucas's shirt and looked into his eyes. "How do you feel?"

Lucas tried to grin. "Like total crap. I want to check on momma and go home with you."

"Let's do it."

Jackson gently touched Sarah's face. She opened her eyes. Her voice was nothing more than a low squeak, "hey."

"Hey, yourself. I've got someone who's very anxious to see you."

Lucas took his mother's hand. "Doc said you going to be fine, but that you need to stay in the hospital for a while. He's taking me home with him. Tomorrow we're going to go over and get Mac."

Sarah was so tired she could hardly lift her hand. She touched Lucas's face. "It's okay, momma, I'm not hurt bad, just a bunch of cuts and bruises."

Sarah forced a smile. "Thank you, Jackson."

"Any time, sweetheart. You relax, and don't worry about a thing, time for you to work on nothing but getting better and when you are better, I'm going take you home with me too."

Chapter 16

Lisa showed up at Jackson's house the day Sarah got hurt. It was extremely late when he came home with Lucas and he found her sitting in the kitchen. He looked up at the clock it was almost one in the morning. He couldn't believe that she was sitting there as if it was an afternoon tea. He almost groaned out loud.

"Lisa, I have to take Lucas's upstairs and get him settled, you can wait if you want, but this may take a while."

"I'll just make some sweet tea while I wait."

Jackson took Lucas's hand. "Come on."

He took Lucas to the guest bedroom next to Colton's. "Let's get you to bed."

"I am really tired and I have to get up early tomorrow."

"You're spending tomorrow in bed."

"I have to get Mac, remember? He'll be hungry and thirsty."

"I'll call Jim Conway and ask him to bring Mac over here. You need to stay put and not be running all over. I'll be right back."

Jackson brought Lucas one of his pajama tops. It was really big on the boy, but he needed to sleep in something for tonight. Tomorrow he would stop by his house and get some clothes for him.

"It's late, crawl under those covers and stay put. If you need anything, just give a call."

Jackson checked on Colton; he was fast asleep with Norman secured in his arms. He closed the door and went to check on Sandy. He was surprised to find her in bed, reading.

He walked in and sat down on the bed. "It's really late, how come you're still up?"

"I couldn't sleep."

"Where's Stormy?"

Sandy pulled the cover back and Stormy's head popped out. Jackson said with a slight smile, "guess she's comfortable enough."

Sandy hugged the puppy to her. "Lisa's downstairs. She sent Mrs. Dutton home."

"I know, I saw her when I came in with Lucas."

"Lucas is here? Why?"

Jackson explained what happened to Sarah and Lucas.

"Is Sarah alright?"

"She will be, but she'll probably be in the hospital for a week or so. Lucas will be staying with us until Sarah gets better and comes home. I intend on bringing her here, she probably shouldn't be alone for a while."

"I think that's a good idea, but what about Lisa?"

"I guess I'll have to go have a talk with her."

Jackson went down to the kitchen where Lisa was still sitting at the table drinking a cup of tea. He didn't say anything to her as he went to the coffee pot and poured himself a cup. He walked over to the table and sat down across from her.

"What are you doing here?"

"I came to see my aunt, took a drive and decided to come see you and the kids."

"I thought we agreed that you would call first."

"Oh, Jackson, what was I supposed to do? Sit outside the door and then call you?"

"Things are very complicated right now, and…………"

There was a knock on the door. Jackson looked up at the clock, it was almost two in the morning and he couldn't imagine who would be knocking at his door at this hour. He got up and answered, he was surprised to see Sheriff Dustin standing on his doorstep.

"Sheriff, come in. Is there something wrong?"

"A lot. We need to talk, Doc."

Jackson went over to the coffee pot, "coffee, Johnny?"

"Please." The Sheriff hung his Stetson on the hook next to the door. He went to the table looked at Lisa. "Ma'am."

"Sheriff Dustin, this is Lisa Fredericks, she was a friend of my late wife."

"Pleasure, ma'am." He turned to Jackson. "This is official business."

"Oh, well, I was just leaving. It's really late. I'll see you tomorrow, Jackson."

"Tomorrow isn't good, Lisa. I'll call you." He said as he escorted her to the door. "It's late, be careful."

Lisa got into her car and slammed the door. She was furious. *How dare he dismiss me like that. It's the bitch.* She was glad that the bitch had an accident and would be kept away from her Jackson. "Maybe she'll do me a favor and just die."

Lisa thought about the Sheriff for only a moment and then dismissed him she had to think because she knew that she was going to have to come up with a plan.

~~~

Jackson placed another cup of coffee in front of the Sheriff. He nodded his thanks. "I'll come right to the point, Doc. We don't think what happened to Sarah Carson and her son was an accident."

Nothing could have surprised Jackson more. His eyes flashed at the Sheriff, he slowly sat down with his fresh cup of coffee. "Why would you think that?"

"Well, sir, I had the car checked because something didn't feel right to me. Alf Morrison over to our police garage checked it out, he was very thorough. Deputy Morrison concluded that the brakes had been tampered with, line was cut almost all the way through. Got any idea who would want to hurt Mrs. Carson?"

"No, none at all. Sarah has no enemies that I know of."

"How's the boy?"

"He's resting. He'll be fine, just has a lot of cuts and bruising."

"I need to talk to him."

"Now? It's the middle of night."

"I want it while it's fresh in his mind."

"I'll go see if he's awake."

Jackson came downstairs with Lucas. The little boy looked small dwarfed by his pajama top. The Sheriff stood up and said, "hey, son, how do you feel?"

"Sore mostly."

"Come sit down with me so we can talk."

Lucas slid onto the chair across from the Sheriff. "Talk about what?"
~~~

"What happened to you and your momma."

Lucas glanced over at Jackson who said, "it's all right, just tell the Sheriff what you remember about the accident."

"I don't remember too much. We were driving along and came to the big mountain, it goes into a curve and momma tried to slow down, but nothing happened when she pressed the brakes. She yelled at me to hold on. We made the first curve okay, but we didn't really make the next one. We hit the side of the mountain bounced off and skidded across to the protective barrier on the right. I guess that's what kept us from going over.

When the car stopped it was quiet, really quiet. I couldn't hear anything until momma started moaning. After that all I could hear was momma, and I couldn't help her. She just kept moaning." Lucas started to cry and Jackson went over to him and picked him up and then sat down in the chair with him. He embraced the boy and spoke quietly to him. He looked up at the Sheriff.

"It's late, and Lucas has been through a terrible ordeal. I think he can't tell you anymore."

"Alright, boy. If you remember anything, give us a call."

"Keep me informed."

"I will, good night, Doc, good night, Lucas. Y'all stay put and I'll let myself out."

Jackson sat with Lucas until he was ready to go to bed. He grinned at the boy, "you, okay?"

"I guess."

"It's really late. I want you to sleep in as late as you possibly can tomorrow. If you have any problems, or the pain increases, call me."

"Are you going to see momma tomorrow?"

"First thing."

"Tell her, tell her that I'm all right."

"I will."

Jackson took Lucas's upstairs and make sure he was comfortable in the bed. "Go to sleep."

Lucas turned over and closed his eyes as Jackson quietly closed the door to the bedroom. He had heard what the Sheriff said about the brakes being tampered with and wondered who would do such a thing. He couldn't think of anyone who would want to hurt them.

Lucas turned when he heard the door open and peered into the dark. "Hey, Lucas. It's just me."

"What are you doing here?"

"I need to make sure that you're alright." Sandy said and jumped up on the bed. Stormy tried to follow her, but couldn't make it. She picked her up and put her next to Lucas. The puppy went directly to him and started washing his face.

"Daddy said you were in an auto accident and you got hurt."

"Momma I had to stay in the hospital. The Doc brought me home with him."

"You want me to leave Stormy with you?"

"No, it's okay. She's much happier being with you."

"I'm tired, if you're okay I'm gonna go back to bed."

"I'm okay, but leave the door open."

Chapter 17

Mandy Sterling looked around her, she wasn't sure where she was. She realized it was some kind of a hospital, and that made sense because she hurt. She hurt badly and discovered if she moved too fast her head screamed at her.

"What the hell happened to me?"

She couldn't remember how she got here, but did remember the gun that was pointed in her direction. She must've gotten shot. The bastard shot her! She reached down to her abdomen and gasped.

"The baby. What happened to the baby?"

The hospital door opened and a tall good-looking man with sandy brown hair and the most gorgeous blue eyes she had ever seen walked in, "good morning."

"Who are you?" she croaked. Her throat was so dry that this was the best she could do.

"I'm Dr. Jackson Shepard, your physician, I took care of you in the emergency room. How are you feeling this morning?"

"Like crap."

Jackson moved closer to the side of Mandy's bed. "Could you be a little more specific?"

"Where's the baby?"

"He's in our intensive care pediatric unit. He was born premature and needs a little help."

"I want to see the baby. It's a him?"

"Yes, it's a boy. How are you feeling today?"

"It doesn't matter."

"Do you know what happened?"

"Yeah, yeah, I do. Paul happened."

"Who's Paul?"

"No one. Maybe you better tell me what happened."

"You were shot several times, and the baby was nicked by a bullet, that's also why he's in the intensive care unit."

"I feel awful. Hurt a lot."

"I'm afraid you're going to hurt for a while. For a long time, there was a question of whether or not you would regain consciousness."

"How long? How long have I been unconscious?"

Jackson checked the IV. "you've been here for several weeks and unfortunately, you are going to have a longer recovery because of the stomach wound. Physical therapy will get you up in a chair today for a short while, and every day you can make more progress. I'll have social service come up and talk to you."

"Do you know who I am?"

"Mandy Sterling. I saw you when you came in 12 days ago."

"Mandy?" Her head felt fuzzy, but she knew her name and it was not Mandy, it was Amanda, and Sterling definitely wasn't her last name. She needed more information. She decided she'd have to play along with whatever this guy said.

"Where am I? What is this place? Am I still in Georgia?"

"Lone Mountain Edge, Georgia. You're in the hospital, Jefferson Memorial.

Amanda had had enough for now. "I'm tired."

"I'm going to order some medicine for you. Rest is very important for your recovery. If you have any problems have the nurse, call me."

After Jackson left Mandy's room, he wrote orders for her. Something was disturbing him about her, she was very unsettling, but he didn't understand exactly what it was that he found so disturbing.

He put Mandy out of his mind and went to see Sarah. He opened the door, grinned and said, "you're looking a lot better than yesterday."

Sarah was sitting in a chair and looked up at Jackson. "I feel like a train wreck. Where's Lucas?"

Jackson pulled up a chair next to her and took her hand, he rubbed it gently. "Lucas is fine, he's at my house safely tucked in bed. I had Mac delivered over to the house yesterday. I hired Avril Patterson and his two sons, Sam and Glenn to work on that old stable behind the house. They're also going to fix the corral. They're almost done, and it looks like a real decent place that any horse would be proud to live in."

"You shouldn't have done that; I'll be out of here soon and back home."

"I wanted to do it. Mac has to have a place to stay too, and when you're discharged, you're coming home with me."

"Jackson, I can't."

"You're going to need help for a while, so you have no options. It's me or you stay in the hospital for a long time."

"That sounds like blackmail."

He winked at her, "I know."

Sarah spent the next two weeks in the hospital and when it was time for her release, Jackson, Lucas, Sarah, and Colton were there to take her home.

Lucas knocked on Sarah's cast. "Does it hurt?"

"No, and stop banging on it."

"Sorry."

When they got home, Jackson insisted she go directly to bed. She objected. "I've been in bed for two weeks; I want to watch a movie."

"Okay, as long as you're not overdoing anything."

"I want a pizza."

Jackson reached over and pulled her into his arms, he gave her a kiss and said, "one purest cheese pizza coming up."

Jackson order three pizzas and gathered the kids. When he came back into the family room Sarah was fast asleep with Stormy.

"Should we wake her up?"

"We better let her sleep, Colton."

~ ~ ~

Alvin paced the small cell and glared at his brother.

"Sit down."

"Were under arrest, Paul, for some bull shit charge."

"Getting caught in a stolen car is not a bull shit charge. Stop worrying, I called Claude."

"Claude? Claude? Are you talking about that dumb ass lawyer, Claude Wolman?"

"That would be the dumb ass lawyer, Alvin, and for your information he's not a dumb ass. Speeding in front of a cop, in a stolen car, that's what's dumb. Shut up for a while. Claude will get us out of this. Just relax."

Alvin threw himself down on the bunk and pulled the pillow over his head. He screamed in frustration.

Claude Wolman looked through the jail bars at Alvin and Paul. "Which one of you two geniuses screwed up this time?"

Paul slowly got up and went over to the bars. He shook hands with his old friend. "That would be Alvin."

"Well, you go before the judge tomorrow morning at nine sharp. If you're lucky, and I wouldn't bet on that, I'll get you bail. You two better make it your business to show up at your next court date. Do we understand each other?"

"Perfectly." Paul pointed to Alvin. "Do you get it?"

"Yeah, I get it, get off my back." He turned to Claude, "just get us the hell out of here."

"Usual fee. I expect payment by next week."

"You've got it."

Paul and Alvin went to court the next morning. They pleaded not guilty and got a bail bondsman. They were back on the street in three hours.

"I'm telling you one more time, don't screw this up." Claude reminded them.

"Got it. Don't worry, we sure don't want to go back there."

"Two months, May 16th, this courthouse, be there." Claude reminded them.

"I got it already." Alvin screamed.

Paul nodded his head, "we'll be here."

Paul and Alvin went back to the apartment. Alvin fell into the couch. "We need to get that money and book out of here."

"We will. I'm going to check the house tomorrow."

"Check it out! Check it out! There's no checking it out. We have to get the money and jewelry and get the hell out, like right now!"

Paul went over to his brother and pulled him up by the shirt. "You need to relax, Alvin. We can't just go barging in there. There are people living in there now. I'll go in at night only if I have to. I'd rather watch them for a while and wait till they go out. Find out their routine. It's safer all around. Do you understand me?"

"Yeah. I understand."

"Then chill out."

Chapter 18

Lucas called to Sandy, "quit stalling and get moving."

"Sarah will be fine. The three of you, go to school."

After the children went out to the bus stop Jackson went upstairs and into Sarah's bedroom. "Mission accomplished. I never knew it took so long to get three little kids off to school. Will you be okay if I make the hospital run?"

"What about the office this afternoon?"

Stormy ran in and attempted to jump up on the bed, she fell, snorted, and let out a small bark. Jackson picked her up and placed her next to Sarah. He leaned over and kissed her.

"I'll be home as soon as possible."

"Stormy and I will be fine. I'm going take a nap and then watch a movie later."

"Call me if you need me."

"Go."

Sarah struggled into her jeans and then tried to put her T-shirt on. She gave up on the T-shirt and took one of Jackson's button-down shirts. The sleeve was big enough to put her cast through. Stormy had followed her from the bedroom to Jackson's bedroom where he sat patiently waiting for her. She turned to the puppy, "I think it's time that we go visit with Mac."

She went out to the renovated barn and over to the corral where Mac was standing under a shade tree. Stormy followed close behind her.

When Max saw Sarah he whinnied a greeting. She opened the gate, when in, and walked over to him placing her arms around him. She introduced the puppy to Mac, and they touch noses, she spent the next half hour with the horse before she got tired and decided it was time to go back to the house.

When she was comfortably seated in the family room, she pulled the cover over both herself and Stormy. She looked down at Stormy and said, "don't tell anyone we went outside to visit with Mac." The puppy twisted her head back and forth as he listened, gave a little snort and then laid down next to her.

While Sarah was visiting with Mac; Paul had snuck into the house and went up to the attic. He was surprised at what he saw. "Someone's been up here." He was referring to the new path that they had made in the center of the room.

Paul went directly to the small jut out room and clicked on his flashlight. He went in and looked at the dolls still sitting at the table. He said to the antique dolls, "Hello again, ladies."

Paul went down to his knees next to the doll with red hair. "This is it, Red, I'm here to take the money and jewelry. I'm so sorry I can't share some of the jewelry with you ladies, but at this point I'm a greedy man and want it all for myself."

He took out his pocket knife and flip the board up, reached down and found nothing. "What the hell!"

Paul kicked the table upsetting the tea party. "Where could it have gone? Where? Nothing. No jewelry, money or guns."

He struggled to get his emotions under control. "This won't solve anything. Someone found that stash, but who? These ass holes who live here? Someone else, who? Dammit, I'm going to have to get out here for now."

A flash of lightning made his escape more urgent. It was going to rain and he had to get out before that happened. He had backtracked and when he got to the bottom of the stairs, he heard a noise that was all too familiar, the growl of the dog. He looked down and saw a floppy eared puppy. He walked past the puppy and silently moved over to the room to his left. He was surprised to see Sarah fast asleep in a lounge chair. The TV was on, but the volume was very low, so low that you almost couldn't hear it. He moved closer; she was a beautiful woman. He thought she must've been some type of accident because she had a cast on her arm and there was slight bruising around her face, that seem to be fading. He just stood watching her for a few minutes until he felt something nip at his ankle. He looked down and saw Stormy.

Paul almost laughed when he saw the puppy standing stiff legged behind him. "Beat it." He said quietly and swiftly moved toward the kitchen. Stormy followed him until he disappeared out the door.

~~~

When Paul returned to the apartment Alvin was waiting for him. "Did you get it? We have to leave right away."

"Relax, no, I didn't get the jewels or the money."

"What! Why the hell not?"

"Because it wasn't there. Someone must've taken it, and I'm betting that whoever took it still has it, and they haven't split. Its someone in that household."

Alan grabbed Paul's arm, "are you sure?"

"No, I'm not sure, but there are people living in that house now. Maybe one of them found it, I'm betting that's what's happened, it only makes sense."
~~~

"Well, let's go get them and make them talk."

"We don't even know who "them" are. I have to do some snooping around and see what I can find out about the family that lives there. I don't know how many people are even in there, I only saw one woman, and a small dog."

"Why didn't you get her to tell you?"

"Maybe she doesn't know, and I couldn't stay around because I didn't know if someone would be walking in at any moment. Whoever took it still has it, and they haven't spent it or would be all over the news. Use your head, Alvin. Think about it."

"I have been thinking about it. Forget the money, forget about the jewelry because we need to get out of here and disappear."

Paul grabbed Alvin by the shirt, "stop! This is going to work out, I just need a little time to make it right. Stop freaking out."

~ ~ ~

There was a sharp knock on the door. Stormy jumped off of the couch and went to see who was invading her territory. She let out a high-pitched bark. Sarah got up and opened the door, she looked down at the dog, "Stormy, stop."

Standing on the other side of the door the Sheriff grinned at her. "Your watch dog got me."

Sarah and the Sheriff were drinking coffee when Jackson walked in. He went over and shook hands with him, "Johnny, it's good to see you again."

"I came to talk to both of you. We have no new clues in our investigation of what happened to Sarah, but we do know that her brake line was deliberately cut

"Why? Who would do that to me?"

"I was hoping you might have an idea. Has anything else unusual happened to you, or your boy?"

"No. Nothing."

"I'm sorry, Miss Sarah, but we just don't have an answer for you. There were no fingerprints, fibers, or anything else. Whoever did this is either very clever, or the luckiest person around."

"I'll be careful, Sheriff, and I'll have a talk with Lucas so that he's aware."

"Anything that disturbs you at all, I want you to give me a call."

"Trust me, Sheriff, you will be my very first call."

Doc, we've also been investigative one Mandy Sterling. The woman is a total mystery. It seems like she just appeared around 13 years ago, before that there is no paper trail. Social Security, driver's license, work history, it all started 13 years ago, but before that nothing."

"What exactly does that mean?"

"That she isn't who she would want us to believe. That girl is hiding something. Who shot her? Who killed her friend, Helen Hardy? And most importantly, who is that baby's father? If we can find the father maybe we can get some more answers I've been up to the hospital to talk to her, she's as closed mouth as they come. She wouldn't even answer simple questions for me. We tracked her down to her last employer, but that was a dead-end. You talked to her, Doc, she said anything to you?"

"No, like you said she is elusive. I'm lucky she response to me at all and when she does it's mostly to be nasty."

"Well, folks, I'm going to go out and see what I can unravel about our mystery woman. Ms. Sarah, any problems don't hesitate to call. Doc, you find out anything about our mystery person, call me. I'll see y'all later. Ms. Sarah, thank you for the coffee."

Jackson smiled at Sarah, "how are you feeling today?"

"I'm fine, and Lucas and I are getting out of your hair, we're going home."

"Sarah......."

"Stop. I've been here almost 3 weeks, its time, and I'm going back to work this Monday."

"Are you sure? Maybe you should take another week off."

"No, and I can't stay with you forever."

Jackson gave her a silly grin, "marry me and you can."

If Sarah felt anything, it was confused, she loved Jackson, that was something she was sure of, but she was reluctant to get married again. She lost her first husband and that had been the most terrible experience in her life and she didn't think she could go through something like that again. She finally had to admit to herself that she was a coward. She was afraid to be hurt like that again. She tried to make light of this offhanded proposal.

"Maybe later, right now I need to pack up and get out of your hair."

He pointed to Stormy. "You're going to make this a very unhappy puppy; you might even break her heart." He gave her a very sad face, "me too."

"You'll both be fine, and I will be coming back to visit Stormy."

Chapter 19

Lucas showed up early, it was seven in the morning, he had ridden his pony, Mac, over because he promised to take Sarah to see what everyone now called, 'Ghost Island'. The original, and real name for the island was 'Faulkner Island', but that name had been abandoned long ago probably before Lucas was even born.

Ghost Island was at the end of a long road, a good two miles from Lone Mountain. No one ever went there anymore because the park was considered haunted, and it had been closed for a very long time. All of the stories surrounding the former amusement park were tragic. Now it stood lonely and abandoned with only the occasional foolish child venturing inside. The authorities had long ago padlocked the gate on the bridge that led to the island.

It was back in the 1930s when Ghost Island was developed into a type of playground for those who could afford it. The island was equipped with all the modern toys of the time. It's pride and joy was a huge Ferris wheel that still stood at the east end of the island. There were also various other types of entertainment offered, slides and swings for the kids, but they were not ordinary ones.

The waterslides were so tall that you had to be brave enough to go up to 50 steps to get to the top. The swing stood on a hill that had headwinds that whipped so strong there was no need for the children to be pushed.

There were many other forms of entertainment, and many other rides. The merry-go-round stood silent in an eerie, long abandoned state. The stately horses seemed to be waiting for their small riders to come back to them.

Lucas had been there alone many times. He enjoyed the peace and quiet it offered him at those times. His favorite thing on the entire island, was this magnificent merry-go-round. He loved the look of the carved horses even though their paint was no longer the once brilliant reds, greens, whites, browns, and golds. This had faded with time. Some of the horses had jewels of various colors that had at one time gleamed in the sun. Half of those were gone. He always wished that he could have seen it when it was new and everything was working properly. He put those thoughts aside and knocked on the door.

Colton flung open the door, he was so excited that he was jumping up and down. Lucas had become his favorite person and he was always happy to see him.

"Hey y'all, are you ready?"

"Come on in." Sandy called.

"Hey, Sandy."

"Daddy already left for the hospital." She held up a cell phone. "We have to check in with him. I made us some sandwiches for later."

"Are you sure you want to go to Ghost Island today. Maybe we should do it another time. It looks like it might rain."

"I want to go." Colton yelled. "Did you bring Mac?"

"He's right outside waiting for us."

Sandy shrugged and stuffed the sandwiches into a bag. "Let's go."

They all piled onto Mac and started down the back roads that would take them to Ghost Island. It was almost an hour before they got to the bridge that led over to Ghost Island.

Lucas pointed to the other side of the bridge. "It's over there. No one is supposed to come here anymore, they say that it's haunted. Jimmy Tallon is supposed to be the ghost that haunts here."

Sandy slid down from Mac and walked over to the barrier that had been placed across the bridge. "Who locked this off?"

Lucas was helping Colton down. "The Town Council. It's been there for a long time, way before I was even born, look how rusty it is."

"Just how old is this place?"

"I think it's from the 30s or maybe the 40s."

"Do you believe that it's haunted by this Jimmy kid?"

"How is it haunted?" Colton wanted to know.

They all decided it was time to eat so they sat down and Sandy passed out sandwiches and soda. Lucas made himself comfortable on the grass. "There was this kid, Jimmy Tallon, he was around our ages, or maybe a little older. Like I said, they claim he's the one that's roaming around here and haunting everything. The story goes that he died on the big Ferris over at the east end of the island. There are actually three Ferris wheels on the property, but the other two are smaller. The Ferris wheel was running when for reasons unknown this Jimmy kid climbs out of his seat and starts going down the side of it. An empty swinging car hit him. The car had broken and was holding on by only half a cable. The kid hit the ground and splattered all over. He was killed right off."

Sandy screwed up her face. "That's just awful."

Colton grinned. "Cool."

"I guess nobody really cared about the Jimmy kid and the fact that he had been killed, probably because he was an orphan and had snuck through the gate. There was an investigation, but in the end, nothing was done." Lucas turned to them and asked, "you still want to go in?"

They both answered, yes.

Lucas made sure that Mac was staked in a grassy area. He patted the horse's shoulder "eat to your hearts content, buddy."

He went back to the barrier and ducked underneath; he was followed by Sandy and Colton. He turned to them and said, "be really careful. This bridge is really old and there's some boards missing on it."

Sandy grabbed Colton's hand as she cautiously moved forward. She was relieved when they finally reached the other side and got off the bridge. It felt like the bridge swayed with every step.

"They originally called this Water Island because of these waters. That was way back before it was called Faulkner Island." Lucas pointed down to the slow-moving water below the bridge.

They walked a quarter-mile before reaching the actual entrance way into the park. It appeared as a huge circle that went from one brick fence wall to the other. On top of the entranceway was a sign that read, "a happy place. The L and C were missing."

There was a chain stretched across the entranceway. There was no way it would stop anyone; they went underneath it with no problem.

Lucas took the first step into the park entrance, Sandy hesitated, but Colton broke free of her grip and ducked under the chain running after Lucas.

Lucas took them over to the merry-go-round. "This is my very favorite thing on Ghost Island. I'll just bet these horses were magnificent when they were new. I sure wish I could've seen them then."

Sandy lightly touched one of the white horses. Time had taken its toll on it, there were bare spots covering part of the face and the rump of the horse. The wood showed through from underneath.

"He is still beautiful."

"I wish I could take them all home with me and make them new again."

"Why don't they restore the park?"

"I guess people are afraid to come here. Everyone believes that the whole thing is haunted."

"Do you?"

Lucas took a deep breath and let it out, "I don't know. Sometimes I think maybe it's haunted. Come on, I want to show you the Ferris wheel."

"Colton make sure you don't wander off. Stay with me or you'll get lost, and we will never find you again."

Colton pointed to his right. "What is that, Lucas?"

"I'm not sure, some kind of car ride."

"They're all rusted."

"Yeah, well, they're just really old and the rust got to them."

Lucas led them to the east end of the park where the massive Ferris wheel sat. He pointed at it, "there it is. Looks kinda lonely today."

Sandy looked up at the long-abandoned Ferris wheel. She had never seen one that huge, it looked like it reached up to the white clouds above it. The years had taken its toll on the structure. The cars that were left had rusted with time, and there were many holes in them. Several had fallen off and lay at the bottom of the wheel and like the rest of the Ferris wheel they were overgrown with foliage and weeds.

All around the base of the wheel lay wild roses and thistle. The herbaceous plant came from the daisy family. Both the roses and the daisies had prickly stems on them. The roses were a variety of colors, but the daisies were only purple and yellow. Butterflies drifted in between the flowers looking for their sweet nectar. The vines had grown up in between the ride to the very top of the wheel. Several of the cars hung crookedly by one end.

Colton's eyes grew wide. "Wow!"

"Y'all be careful of those thorn plants at the bottom because they bite. It's been a long time since I've been here."

"Lucas, do you think any of these rides work anymore?"

"Maybe, but this park would need a lot of repairs to be operative again."

Suddenly, the wind changed and it became cold, there was a crack of thunder that seem to rumble across the ground. It felt like the ground had moved underneath their feet. Lucas looked up, "I think we better get going. It's going to rain, and this property will get muddy really fast."

They ran through the park and out the entranceway, but by the time they got back to the bridge it was pouring. "Sandy, grab Colton's hand." Lucas took his other hand. "Let's go easy. We have to get across the bridge as fast as we can."

Below them the quiet stream raged with rushing water; the wind had picked up even more which made crossing the bridge difficult. Lucas briefly watched the water go by underneath them.

He didn't want to fall in because he didn't know if he could swim well enough to survive it. "Take it slow." He yelled into the wind.

Sandy watched every step she took and hung on to Colton, she didn't want him to slip. They came to where several planks were missing. What had seemed an easy task was now a hazardous experience; the boards were getting more slippery and Sandy had already fallen once.

Just as they got to the end of the bridge Sandy slipped again taking Colton down with her. Lucas grabbed Colton's belt and pulled him onto the grass. He went back to help Sandy who was gripping the edge of the bridge and part of the grassy bank. She was hanging half on and half off.

He flung himself down on the ground and yelled, "take my hand and I'll pull you up."

Lucas glanced down at the swiftly moving waters. Sandy's feet were half in there and she was swaying back and forth with the current which made it harder to keep his grip on her. He could feel himself being pulled forward by inches. He let go of the bridges post and took hold of Sandy's arms with both of his hands. He pulled with all his strength. He wasn't going to let go, and he wasn't going to let the raging river below take her. If she went into the water he would lose her, she would be taken by the river below, she would die. He pulled with all his strength.

Lucas grunted with the effort of holding onto Sandy. "Try to pull yourself up." He screamed into the wind.

Colton had thrown his body across Lucas's legs to help anchor him.

Sandy pulled and managed to get a foot out of the water. She tried to brace herself against the bank, but the sand crumbled under her and her foot splashed back into the water. The water was pulling at her and it felt like a huge force was trying to pull her down. She wanted to scream, but found she had no voice, terror was pulling at her mind.

"Sandy, you have to hold on."

Lucas applied as much force against the bank as he could and she slowly edged out of the water. Once her feet were free, he pulled back and she tumbled onto the grass with him. He gathered her up into his arms and they both lay on the grass panting. Sandy gave in to her motions and started to cry. Lucas held her tight and waited for her to calm.

He looked down into her face and said, "Don't cry anymore. We've got enough water to deal with here."

She started to hick up and laugh. "I think you're right."

Lucas struggled to his feet and then helped Sandy up. Colton stood in the rain. "Let's go home."

Lucas boosted Sandy onto Mac, and then helped Colton. "I'm going to walk him so he doesn't slip. This ground is really muddy." It would take them a long time to return to Sandy's house. The road was so thick with mud that it tore it Lucas's shoes. He finally took his tennis shoes off and handed them to Colton. He actually got better traction in bare feet.

When they got back to the house Lucas told them to go on in. "I'll take care of Mac and be right up."

The wind had picked up even more and the rain was coming down faster. It was a cold rain. The sky illuminated with a color that made it look like it was on fire, he had never seen anything like it, it was brilliant and for several seconds the sky seemed like it was burning. Loud claps of thunder followed, and then the sky darkened once again.

He put Mac in a stall, grabbed a rag and wiped him down. When he was done, he went into the tack room and came back with a blanket. He covered the pony and make sure that he was comfortable. Before Lucas left, he made sure Mac had enough to eat and access to water. He closed all the windows to keep the cold out, went back and gently patted the pony's neck. "I'll come by later and check on you."

When he left the small barn, he closed the door and sprinted across to the house. He went in the kitchen and stripped off his wet shirt. Sandy walked into the kitchen with a towel, she had taken a fast shower and pulled on warm clothes. She handed Lucas the towel.

"You should probably go take a bath, or shower."

"Yeah, I'm almost about to freeze."

"I can get you one of daddy's T-shirts, and maybe a pair of his sweatpants."

"It's okay, I left some of my clothes here. Where's Colton?"

"He's in the tub."

"I'll go up and use my bedroom." In the short time Lucas had lived with the Shepards he considered the bedroom and bath he used as his. "I'll be down shortly."

"I'll make some hot chocolate."

Lucas walked into the kitchen in the old jeans and T-shirt he had left behind. "I don't have any shoes, mine are soaked."

"Sit down. I made the chocolate."

"This is really good. I was cold."

Colton and Stormy came running into the kitchen, Stormy skidded to a stop.

"She doesn't like storms and neither do I."

"It's just a bunch of noise. Sandy made some chocolate come and have some. That storm is outside and were inside so it can't hurt us."

"You try to tell that to Stormy. She doesn't like the noise it makes."

Lucas slid down to the floor and pulled the puppy into his lap. She was shaking and whimpering. "I think we better go into the TV room and watch a movie. Maybe that'll take Stormy's attention off of what's going on."

The telephone rang just as they were getting settled into the TV room. Sandy went to answer it.

"Hey, daddy."

"Is everyone all right? That's a bad storm that's going on out there. Alerts have been issued all over town."

"Were all fine. We're just going to watch a movie. We got really wet coming home........."

"Where did you go?"

"We rode Mac around. When are you coming home? Is Sarah coming with you?"

"Yes, Sarah's coming home with me, but as long as you kids are all right were going to wait out some of the storm here."

"Were okay, and if we get hungry, I can make sandwiches."

"Stay in the house, no more going out."

"We won't."

"If you need anything, call me."

"Don't worry, we're just going to watch a movie."

"Love you."

"Love you too, daddy."

It took Colton all of five minutes to fall asleep. Even Stormy was asleep in a few minutes, she had curled up between Sandy and Lucas on the couch. Sandy threw a blanket over Colton and the puppy.

"That park may or may not be haunted, but it's downright dangerous. I thought I was going to be taken off by that river."

"I would never have let go."

"It really scared me. I thought I would be swept away and drowned."

"That didn't happen, so don't even think about it."

~~~

Sarah and Jackson went down to the hospital cafeteria to get something to eat. It seemed like everyone left in the hospital had the same idea. The cafeteria was filled. They took a tray and ordered.

"There's a table over there."

They sat down together, but didn't talk. When they were finished Sarah laughed. "I didn't know I was that hungry."

"Me either."

They each had a cup of coffee and never realized that they were being watched. Lisa sat several tables down from them. She was dressed in a nurse's uniform and had a hoodie that zipped up. A lot of second shifters had come in from the rain dressed the same way, so she didn't stand out.
~~~

Lisa kept her head down and watched as they finished their coffee. She almost bolted from the table when Jackson reached over and placed his hand over Sarah's. "That Bitch" she said under her breath and forced herself to stay seated, but all she really wanted to do was go over there and rip Jackson away from her.

The rain had almost stopped, Lisa followed Jackson and Sarah to the hospital emergency room exit. She stood in the shadow and watch them leave. She stayed a good distance away as she watched them so they wouldn't see her.

"I'll follow you." Sarah said. "I have to collect Lucas."

"He could stay, so can you."

"Tomorrow is a school day, remember?"

"All right, I'll meet you at my mystery house." Jackson turned back to Sarah. "Are you off tomorrow?"

"Yes, Monday and Saturday this week."

"Come over. I've got a whole lot of attic to go through and you might find something you can't live without."

Sarah couldn't help but laugh. "How can I resist an offer like that? Is noon all right, I'm really tired and would like to sleep in"

"Noon, it is."

Chapter 20

Paul walked into Jefferson Memorial through the emergency room entrance. There were a lot of people seated throughout the waiting room. An older woman was bent over a wheelchair moaning. A middle-aged man slumped into a chair holding a towel to his face, it was tinged with blood. A couple holding a baby were talking to the nurse in charge. He walked past a woman who was pushing a wheelchair and dragging a blanket behind her. A middle-aged woman sat in a chair, rocking back and forth and calling to someone named Marvin. There were two small children arguing over some kind of a toy, the woman seated next to them yelled for them to stop.

A man rushed in and ran to the nurse who was talking to the couple with the baby. He had his hand across his abdomen, blood was dripping through his fingers. Just as he reached the nurse, another man sitting in a wheelchair tipped over and hit the floor.

Several employees came running out from the back of the emergency room to help with the chaos. In the disorder and confusion, Paul was unnoticed as he went through the emergency room lobby and into the hospital. It was late and the entire hospital was in what they called a brown down. All the lights had been dimmed as the hospital went into sleep mode. The hallway he walked down was deserted, he saw a sign that said physicians lounge, opened the door and went in. He found a lab coat thrown over a couch, picked it up and put it on. It wasn't an exact fit, actually it was too big for him but it would work, he walked out of the lounge in the white coat. He buttoned it up and headed for the elevator, when he got there, he went in and pressed the third floor.

Paul had called the hospital earlier in the day and asked for Mandy Sterling's room number. He strolled down the third-floor hallway and into room 324. When he went into the room, he saw Mandy lying still in the bed. As he stared at her she turned over onto her back and moaned. Quietly, he went to the bed and looked down, he felt nothing for her, not even a small amount of compassion.

In his mind the problem with Mandy was she knew too much about him. She could nail him for the robbery and he wasn't going to jail because she couldn't keep her mouth shut. He knew she would eventually tell. If she thought she could get out of trouble she would tell everything. The solution was simple, he would have to kill her because there was no other way. He went to the other side of the bed and took the spare pillow that was lying on the chair next to it. Just as he was lifting the pillow, a light from the hallway flooded the room. He quickly fluffed the pillow, lifted Mandy's head and place it underneath her. He was surprised she didn't wake up, but figured she had been sedated.

"Doctor??"

"I was just going home and came to check on Ms. Sterling."

"I don't believe we've met."

"I'm Dr. Cruz, I've just partnered with Dr. Shepard, so I'm new to everyone."

"I'm Nurse Dodge, I work the night shift, it's a pleasure to meet you. Mandy seems to be doing well."

He walked over and said, "thank you, Nurse Dodge."

Paul quickly walked down the hall and got on the elevator. Jackson Shepard was the only name he could think of and he only knew that because he researched the house on Mockingbird Lane. He also knew that Mandy Sterling was actually Amanda Lansing. If you knew how to use it the Internet was a wonderful thing. He learned from it everything that happened at Mockingbird Lane.

~~~

It was a cold rainy November night when Alice Jean Lansing decided to leave and take her son, Bobby Joe. She had a huge fight with her husband, Alvin that morning. They had been arguing for days about anything and everything. They screamed at each other, slammed doors, and snarled anytime they passed each other in the hall. She screamed at him that she was going to get a divorce and he should get the hell out. He refused. She decided to get a lawyer and have him forced out of the house, until then she would take Bobby Joe and find a place for them. The argument turned violent and she did just what she said, she left with Bobby Joe.

Bobby Joe Lansing was found dead. He was lying on the bank of Burns River. It was determined that he had been suffocated and dumped there approximately two days before. A statewide search for Alice Jean found nothing. It seemed like she had disappeared into the world's darkness.

Amanda and her father were investigated, she claimed that she had no idea why her mother had left her behind and took only her brother. She also didn't understand why her mother would kill her brother, if she had. They had always been close, much closer than Amanda had ever been to her mother.

It was the father who was convinced that she killed the boy because she had filed for divorce and didn't want him to have any access to his son. He told the Sheriff if he found Alice Jean, they would find Bobby Joe's killer.

Two weeks later, Alvin Lansing was found hanging in the upstairs foyer. It was deemed that he committed suicide. Amanda claimed her father was so distraught that he had decided to kill himself.
~~~

Two days later she walked away from the house, and like her mother, disappeared, until now.

Paul knew her true identity, and instead of killing her maybe he could use it against her.

Chapter 21

"Colton, hurry up, we have to go or we will be late for school."

"Who cares? I'm coming."

Colton was sitting on the floor of his bedroom; he pulled his soldier box to him. In it he kept his army men, he had green, red, blue, and yellow soldiers. He would spend hours making play forts all around his bedroom and positioning his various armies, but today they had a more important job to do. He put all of the jewelry he had found up in the attic into the bottom of the soldier box. He looked at the 2-carat diamond ring he had in his hand and then dropped it into the box. He carefully placed all of his various armies on top.

"You guys guard our treasure while I'm gone."

Sandy yelled again from the bottom of the stairs. "Colton!"

"Okay, Sandy, I'm coming."

He didn't have time to find a place for the money he found, so he opened his sock drawer, threw all of them on the floor and dumped the $7000 into it. He briefly wondered where all the money came from, but dismissed it immediately. It was now his treasure. He gathered up all the socks and put them on top of the money. When he slammed the drawer, he noticed a $10 bill laying on the floor. He jammed that into his pocket, grabbed his books, stopped, and reached up to pat his horse, Buck. Sandy called again and he ran down the stairs.

~~~
~~~

Sarah showed up exactly at noon. Jackson opened the door, pulled her into his arms and kissed her. He looked deep into her eyes and said, "marry me."

"I can't, we have an attic to de-clutter, but I will have lunch with you."

After lunch they went up to the attic, he flipped on the lights and looked around. "I have to get some better lighting up here."

Sarah looked into the sea of things that were lining the entire attic. They had only hit the tip of this iceberg; this would take a long time to complete.

"Do you even know what you're going to do with all this stuff?"

"Throw out the junk." He pointed to the stack of black garbage bags he had brought at the hardware store. "What's good, I'll donate."

"This is going to take a long time and a lot of work to get through."

"That's okay. In a way I've been having fun with it. Sometimes I actually find it relaxing. See that pile of boxes over there? I found a lot of sheets and towels in them. They're all in their original packaging. They have never been opened or used. There are also four boxes of untouched toys, still brand-new in the wrappers."

"What do you want to keep, and what do you want to toss?"

"If you see anything you want, take it. Anything broken, or obvious junk just toss it."

Sarah looked over in the corner where the huge wooden horse had been only yesterday. "What happened to the horse?"

"Buck. He now has a home in Colton's bedroom. Mike Poole, from the hospital came over and helped me move him down there."

"That's great, because I was wondering how we were going to get him down those stairs."

"It wasn't an easy job; he was so big, he barely fit."

They both went to different places in the attic and worked in silence for over an hour until Sarah called out, "Jackson, come over here."

"Where is here?"

"I'm all the way in the back, there's some kind of a door over here behind a huge bed."

Jackson made his way through several piles of boxes that had been pushed to the side. "Be careful," Sarah yelled out, "there's some kind of pole lying on the floor."

When he found Sarah, he kissed her. "I'm here at your beckon call."

"Just look at this beautiful bed I found. It's really old, it has to have been up here for a very long time."

He looked at the headboard of the bed, Sarah was right, it was beautiful.

It was probably a bed that was made around 1920, next to it stood a matching huge dresser. Each piece was hand carved in walnut. The headboard was inlaid with various colors going from light to dark wood. Mother-of-pearl circles dotted the entire headboard on the top. There were carved cherubs, c-scrolls, flowers, and rocailles throughout the huge headboard. There were two tall posters on the footboard. The footboard was not as ornate, but was beautifully hand carved. It was made in three pieces, dark in the middle with two lighter ends. The two end pieces had designs of rocailles throughout while the middle piece alternated light and dark boards.

The dresser was also adorned with several matching cherubs. It had two sections, the lower had three large drawers while the top portion had only two. On each side of the top portion were additional drawers the length of the two accompanying drawers next to them. On the top sat the cherubs. They were inlaid with two separate dark and light tones. Everything was set in a round value.

"It is beautiful."

"You have an empty bedroom downstairs; we should put this set in there."

"I'd have to get a new mattress for it because even Stormy wouldn't sleep on that old thing."

At the mention of his name Stormy lifted her head. She was back on the chair that she had found last time they were up here. "I guess I'll have to put that chair downstairs because Stormy has taken a real liking to it."

Jackson and Sarah spent the entire afternoon going through different items they found. When Jackson opened the door behind the bed, he found another room that was filled with even more stuff. When they decided to call it quits, he shook his head, "doesn't look much different. Maybe I should call someone into just clean everything out."

"You don't want to do that. I think this is fun."

He looked at her like she was crazy. "Are you serious?"

"Yes, and look at what I found."

Sarah held up a small piece of stained glass and he had to admit it was unique. It was square, maybe 10 inches high by 12 wide. He turned his head and looked at it again. "What is it?"

"Some kind of stained-glass floral accent mirror. See the mirrored piece behind the flowers?"

"I do."

"Just look at the pretty colors that swirl around the center flower. I just love the blues and yellows that embrace the pink flowers."

"You can barely see the mirror. What good is it?"

"You are impossible. It's an art piece, not a mirror."

Jackson grunted at her indignation. He shrugged, "if you like it, take it."

~~~

Lucas couldn't wait until school was over, another hour and they would be turned loose. He sighed, looked at the clock and said, "it can't be soon enough.

"Is there something you would like to share with the class, Mr. Carson?" Asked Mrs. Watson.

"No, ma'am, I think it's best if I don't say anything at all."

"Oh, no, Mr. Carson, you can tell the class about the Underground Railroad and what its function was."

"The Underground Railroad was…………"

"You will stand while addressing the class."

Lucas dragged himself out of his seat. "Dammit." He said under his breath and he stood next to his desk. He looked out the window while he recited, "the Underground Railroad was established to help black people to escape during the Civil War. They had been forced into slavery and would do anything to escape that faith. It was an entire network of people and hideouts that help slaves from the South escape up to the North. A man name Isaac Hopper, he was a Quaker man, he was the one who got it started".
~~~

Lucas grinned to himself. "They had this train that was under the ground. They built long tunnels running all the way to New York City, so people could ride on it comfortably. They also poked holes in the ground so that the smoke could get out and not choke everyone."

Most of the kids knew better and laughed. Mrs. Mason turned red. "That's enough, Lucas Carson!" She yelled as loud as her squeaky voice would allow. "The class is dismissed with the exception of Lucas Carson.

Sandy and Colton sat down on the steps outside to wait for Lucas. All the other kids had already bolted and were probably halfway home by now.

"Why is Lucas so late?"

"Mrs. Mason kept him after."

"Oh. Okay."

Sandy put her arm around her brother. "He should be out soon."

Lucas tapped Sandy on the shoulder, she turned and asked, "what happened?"

"She got me for telling lies."

"I thought it was funny."

"Hey, y'all, let's go have a soda."

"You need money for that, and I don't have any."

"I do, Sandy."

Colton dug into his pants pocket and pulled out the crumble $10 bill. He pressed it flat against his jeans and held it up. Sandy took the bill from him and examined it. "Where did you get a $10 bill?"

"Found it."

"Where?"

Colton shrugged. "Somewhere."

She flicked him on the head with her finger. "That's not an answer. Where did you get it?"

"I told you. I found it. I'm going to Cooper's for a soda and y'all can come if you want to, or go home."

"You're not supposed to go anywhere alone."

They walked together over to Cooper's drugs. In the front of the store there was a pharmacy and rows of products ranging from aspirin to foot powder. In the middle, there were comic books and toys. Farther down there were home products, hand towels, drinking glasses, assorted things like wrapping paper, cards and even pots and pans.

At the very end of Cooper's drugstore was the soda bar where you could get ice cream floats, sodas, banana splits, or just plain ice cream. They sat on a bar stool in front of the counter.

"Hey, Timmy." Lucas called.

Timmy Gacy was older than Lucas, he was 15. He also had been a coach on his baseball team, the Badgers, until this year. Lucas was surprised to see him working at Cooper's.

The boy turned from the cash register and smiled, "hey, Lucas, how's things going with the Badgers?"

"Okay, we won our last three games. Is this why you don't come by anymore because you're working for Cooper?"

"Yeah, I'm trying to help my daddy out. Momma's been sick all year and she can't work. Debbie and Lucy stay with her while me and daddy are working."

Debbie and Lucy were his two younger sisters. Lucy was eight, and Debbie and seven.

"Sorry about your momma." He muttered.

"It's just the way it is. Hey, what can I get y'all?"

"A root beer float."

"What's that?" Colton wanted to know.

Lucas turned to him and said, "just about the best thing you'll ever taste, have one. You have one too, Sandy. Oh, Timmy, these are my friends, Sandy and Colton Shepard."

"Hey, I know your daddy, he takes care of my momma."

"Then she'll get better." Colton advised him.

"Make that three root beer floats."

"I'm paying." Colton said and laid the still crumble $10 bill on the counter.

Sandy had to agree that the root beer float was the best soda she had ever had. Lucas laughed, "I can't believe you never had one before."

"Never did."

They were walking out when Timmy called Colton back. "You forgot your change." He handed Colton $6.35. Colton looked at the money in his hand and took the five-dollar bill and handed it back to Timmy. "What's this for?"

"A tip."

"Thanks, but that's way too much. I can't take this."

"Yes, you can, it's a tip." Colton yelled and ran to catch up with Sandy and Lucas.

"Hurry it up or you'll get lost. What were you doing?"

"I went back to give Timmy a tip."

Colton dropped the quarter and bent to pick it up. He shoved the left over dollar, quarter and dime into his jeans.

"How much of a tip did you leave?" Sandy asked expecting him to say a dime.

"Five dollars."

"Why did you leave so much?" Lucas asked.

"Because he's got a sick momma and he needs it, I don't."

Sandy half smiled at him. "That was really nice, Colton."

Chapter 22

Amanda woke up and looked around. She groaned because moving really hurt. She decided she had to get outta here before they killed her. The damn physical therapy was enough to kill her. All she wanted right now was to be left alone. She had a strange dream that Paul had come to visit her, but knew that was impossible and dismissed it. He didn't even know where she was at, or if she was alive. She needed to get out, she wanted to take the baby with her but realized she couldn't. She would be lucky to take care of herself right now. She still has one friend in town, if she still lived here and if she was willing to help her out.

Amanda decided to go tonight, she would leave the kid and come back for him later. Baby Jackson Sterling as he was being called would be better off for now without her.

She thought about the baby, they had let her see him twice. He was so tiny and still had oxygen to help him breathe. She actually thought he looks somewhat ugly with his wrinkled skin and tiny feet pumping back and forth. The nurse wanted her to try and breast-feed him. She wanted no part of that and made it clear to them that it would not be happening.

She couldn't worry about the kid right now, and wondered if she really did want to come back for him. Now, she had to leave, she hurt, but was ambulatory and figured if she could make it to Nancy, she would stay with her until she completely recovered.

Amanda was taken by wheelchair back to her room. After the aide left, she went to the phone and called information to ask for Nancy Harris's address and phone number.

When she received the number, she called it. Nancy answered immediately. "Girl, you just come on over, or better yet I'll pick you up."

"I really appreciated it, Nan, I'll explain everything to you when I see you."

"Give me an hour."

Amanda was waiting outside for Nancy and quickly got into the car before anyone could see her. The parking lot was dark and quiet and she was sure that they had not been observed as they left the hospital.

~~~

It was Friday, and Sarah had come back to help Jackson, he took eight more bags out to the curb. He reflected that it hardly put a dent in the attic problem. Just as he turned to go back to the house a flashy red convertible was driving up. Lisa blew her horn and waved at him. He groaned and wondered what she was doing here and why she didn't understand, call first.

Lisa stopped her car, jumped out and walked briskly over to him. She saw Sarah out of the corner of her eye and threw herself into Jackson's arms. He had no choice but to embrace or they both would've wound up on the ground. She gave him a full kiss on the mouth. He gently pushed her away.

"You don't know how I've missed you." As a quick afterthought she added, "and the children, of course, where are they?"

"Lisa, what are you doing here?"

"I came to see you." She pouted. "It's been so long, and I had business up in this area, so I just dropped by."
~~~

Sarah came out and went over to the pile of junk from the attic. She placed the two bags she was carrying down and then went to join them.

"Hello, Lisa."

"Oh, hello, Sally, isn't it?"

"Sarah."

"Of course."

"Sarah and I are very busy right now, this is not a good time, Lisa."

"I just wanted to see you and the kids. Where did you say they were?"

"School. It's a school day." Jackson's cell phone rang. He answered, "Dr. Shepard."

He listened for a few minutes and then said, "call the Sheriff. She's not well enough to go far. What about the baby?"

He listened again and said, "please keep me informed and have hospital security keep a watch on the baby. If the Sheriff needs me, I'm at home. Thank you."

Sarah completely ignored Lisa. "What happened?"

"Mandy Sterling took off."

"What about the baby?"

"He's fine. Still in the peds unit, evidently, she left without him."

"Why that's just terrible." Lisa said in an exasperated voice. "How could anyone leave their baby behind?"

"It would've been a disaster for the baby if she had taken him with her."

Lisa completely switched the subject back to her. "Are you going to ask me in for coffee?"

Jackson was about to say no when Sarah said, "it's time for a break. I'll make the coffee."

Lisa was dressed in a leopard outfit, Sarah thought she looked like the predator that she was and gave a short laugh. Jackson glanced at her and she shook her head before going over to the coffee maker. He sat down at the table with Lisa while Sarah started the coffee. She brought the coffee over to the table and placed a cup in front of both of them.

"I'm going back upstairs so you two can talk. There's still a lot to do up there."

Before Jackson could utter a word, she was gone, but not before she gave him a sympathetic grin. She knew exactly what Lisa was trying to do.

Jackson turned to Lisa, "I have told you before that you have to call and not just show up here."

"I haven't seen you in so long, and I was in the area, now you're scolding me."

Jackson didn't want her here, in fact, he didn't want her to ever come back. He wanted her completely out of his life and had deliberately not called or made any type of contact with her. He decided it was time to get tough. "Lisa, I don't want to hurt you, but you were my wife's friend and I have no romantic interest in you something that I believe you want and I can't do."

Lisa jumped up from the chair, it crashed to the floor. "I only want to be your friend, a friend to Mary's children and you constantly reject me." She screamed and then softened immediately when she realized that this was the wrong approach. "Jackson, just give us a chance. I can make you very happy. I will even make the kids happy. I'll give you anything you want."

She had draped herself across his back. He stood up so she had to let go of him. He took a step backwards. "It won't happen between us. You need to find someone else, someone who can return your feelings. Go, have a happy life and find that someone who is willing to share himself with you. That person cannot be me."

Lisa was furious and wanted to scream. *That Bitch, Sarah, wasn't for him.* She was the only one for him, and she had to convince him of that. She fought to control herself. "I'm sorry you feel that way, we could've been very good together. You should have given it a chance. You know my number, call me, at any time, and I will come."

Lisa turned and left, she got into her car and tore down the driveway before racing down the road.

Jackson was exhausted and sat down in the chair, when he turned to the doorway Sarah was there.

"Wow, she is possessed."

"I should've told her sooner. I didn't mean to lead her on in any way."

"I don't think that you did."

Lisa was speeding down the road when she came up with a plan. She laughed wildly, stripped off her scarf and let it fly in the wind. She would start her plan tonight."

~ ~ ~

Amanda was sitting comfortably on her friend, Nancy's couch. She had a soft throw and a whiskey sour in front of her. She had given Nancy most of the details about what had happened to her.

"What are you going to do now?"

"Nancy, that is a very good question, one that I don't have an answer for."

Nancy took another drink; she was having whiskey straight up. "You have to get this guy to give you part of the money he stole. It's only fair." She got up, came back with another whiskey sour and placed in front of Amanda. "What about the kid?"

"I don't know what I'm going to do about the kid. He's sickly and look at me, I thought I wanted him, but now I'm not so sure. I guess I'll just have to see how things work out." She downed the drink and held out the glass. "I'm going to contact Paul."

"The guy who shot you?"

"Paul didn't shoot me, that prick, Stanley Richards, did it because I didn't move fast enough to suit him."

"Do you even know where this Paul is?"

"It shouldn't be hard to find him. He and his crummy brother are probably still at that crappy apartment."

~~~

While Amanda and Nancy were making plans for Paul, he was watching the Shepards. He knew about Dr. Shepard and his two kids, but the woman was new to him, he discovered that she had a kid also. The little group seemed real cozy together. He had watched their comings and goings for the last few weeks.

The Doc was off to the hospital around 8 AM every day and then to his office, usually he returned around 6:30 in the evening.
~~~

The kids left for school at the same time as the Doc, and came home about three in the afternoon. They always stayed around the house. Usually the other kid, the one who belonged to the woman, was with them.

He had also seen another woman sneaking round the house. She looked about 30, had black hair, and well-built. He knew she was up to no good. He laughed heartily, "my kind of woman."

Everyone was gone right now, but he wasn't ready to go in. Lisa had just arrived, and Paul looked at his watch. It was 2 P. M. He watched as she opened the window on the side of the house and climbed in.

Lisa went through the window she always used to get into the house, and then up to the attic. She could see some of the progression Jackson had made up there, but there was still plenty of places to hide if she had to. She sat in the chair Stormy always occupied. Now it was a waiting game. She heard the children when they came home and moved over to a cluttered spot in the back of the attic just in case, they came up here. She made herself comfortable and waited.

Sarah picked up Lucas and they went home. Jackson got the kids ready for bed because he had a hard day and wanted to retire early. He stretched out on his bed and instantly fell asleep. By 9 PM everyone in the household was asleep.

Lisa waited until she heard no activities downstairs, then she crept down from the attic. She dropped a black silk square of material over her head and went to Sandy's bedroom.

"Savanna Shepard," she called in a weary voice. "I have come for you.................. "

Stormy jumped up and issued a puppy growl before ducking back under the covers. It woke Sandy up. "What? Stormy?"

"Get out, Savanna Shepard. Go back to Atlanta."

Sandy looked up and saw a floating figure coming towards her. Stormy who plastered himself against her was violently shaking and whimpering.

"Get out." The dark figure called again.

Sandy mustarded every ounce of courage that she had, picked up the lamp on the small dresser next to her and threw it as hard as she could, the black figure yelped. Sandy screamed.

When Jackson ran into the bedroom, he found Sandy cowering in bed with Stormy securely in her grasp. "It was here." She said in a quavering voice.

He went over and pulled both his child and the dog to him. "What happened?"

"Daddy, something was in here. I saw it. Stormy saw it. It's the ghost in this house."

Jackson got up and turned on the lights. Sandy's smashed lamp was lying near the bedroom door. He bent down to get a better look, there was blood on the pieces that lay around the floor. "Whoever was in here was no ghost. Come over here, Sandy."

Sandy went over to her father, he pointed down at the smashed lamp. She saw the red blood. "Is that blood?"

"Yes, get your robe on. I'm calling the Sheriff."

Colton, who could sleep through a hurricane never woke up. Jackson and Sandy followed the blood trail down the stairs and over to the window that someone had left wide open.

"This was no ghost."

Sheriff Dunton and Deputy Rance Longman were at the house in 15 minutes. Being a small town there was no night shift at the

Sheriff's office and the call went directly to their home? The Sheriff had thrown jeans on over his pajamas and wore his coat with the Sheriff's badge pinned to it.

The Sheriff and Deputy Longman walked through Sandy's bedroom and like Jackson had done they followed the blood trail to the window.

"You've got an intruder all right. He looked over at Sandy who was curled on the couch with Stormy. He walked over, smiled at the little girl and asked, "are you alright, Sandy?"

"Yes, sir. It just scared me because I thought it was a ghost."

"This was no ghost. Doc, do you know why anyone would want to break in here?"

"No, but this isn't the first time we've had a visit from Sandy's ghost."

"Someone broke in before?"

"Yes, sir, I thought Sandy was having nightmares when she saw a black figure in her bedroom. It's happened twice before."

The Sheriff sat down across from Sandy and Stormy. Deputy Longman was busy collecting evidence and taking pictures.

"Can you tell me exactly what happened?"

"You mean when I thought I was having bad dreams?"

"Yes."

"It was dark, so I didn't see whatever it was clearly. It talked to me."

"What did it say? Did you recognize the voice?"

Sandy closed her eyes and brought back the image of the dark figure. "It was all in black so it was hard to see it. It looked kinda wavy and moved slow. It growled at me mostly, but this time it said, "get out or you'll die. Go back to Atlanta."

Jackson had been listening to all that Sandy was saying. "Are you sure it said go back to Atlanta?"

"I'm sure. I thought that was really a funny thing for it to say to me. It's really scary, Sheriff."

The Sheriff reached over and lightly touched her cheek, "don't you fret, I'll get whoever did this. Y'all go up to bed and don't worry."

"Daddy, can me and Stormy sleep with you?"

Jackson picked her up kissed her cheek and said, "go on up and I'll be there soon."

After Sandy left Jackson told the Sheriff he knew who Sandy's ghost was.

<div style="text-align: center">~~~</div>

Lisa wrapped the scarf around the cut on her arm. "That damn kid, what the hell's wrong with her throwing that lamp at me? Bitch!" She screamed and hit the steering wheel with her other hand.

Lisa stopped about 4 miles from Jackson's house to examine her arm. It was dark, but she could see that the cut was deep and it hadn't stopped bleeding. She made the scarf tighter which slowed the bleeding down, she needed to be stitched up. She knew she couldn't show up at the hospital, not with Jackson being on call for the emergency room. She would have to drive all the way to Atlanta and go to a hospital there. "Damn that kid."

Chapter 23

The Sheriff studied Jackson. "How would you know who broke into your house?"

"Because she used the phrase, 'go back to Atlanta.' Lisa Fredericks, she has an aunt who lives about 20 miles from here in Marrow. She was a friend of my deceased wife."

"Why would she terrorize your child?"

"I think we're going to need coffee for this one, Johnny."

While they drank the coffee Jackson explained to the Sheriff and Deputy Longman about Lisa. "She's in love with me and wants me to come back to Atlanta with her."

"I guess I have to ask you this question, are you in love with her? Did you lead her on in any way?"

"No, in fact, I told her to go find someone else. I asked her not to come back here."

"I'll have her picked up and questioned, but we may not be able to hold her. There isn't too much evidence here and even if the blood is a match.........."

"I know, half the population could have the same blood type."

"If it is her, maybe we can put a scare into her and she'll leave y'all alone. In the meantime, I suggest you get a security system so if someone enters, you'll know about it."

"Good idea."

"Rance and I will do some drive-byes, a little more police presence might help."

Jackson shook hands with both the Sheriff and Deputy Longman, "thank you for your help."

"We'll be talking to you."

~~~

Colton went to get a pair of socks and looked down at all the money in his drawer. "This hiding place sucks."

He walked around the room searching for a better place, but couldn't think of one. He went to the closet, dumped out his new dress shoes and took the box. He neatly placed the stacks of money into the shoebox. Some of them were still in the wrappers from the bank. It was the jewelry stores cash for the month and it hadn't been used yet.

Colton sat down on the bed and placed the shoebox next to him. He had to think. "I could take it back up to the attic." He quickly rejected that idea because if he had it up there, he might forget where he put it. There was too much stuff.

Colton smiled, he had come up with the Perfect Place, Dodge City.

When he came back upstairs, Sandy and his father were eating breakfast. Jackson grinned at him, "you better get a move on. Didn't you hear me call?"

"No, I was visiting Dodge City."

~~~

The next morning, Jackson asked his children to join him in the family room. He was surprised when Lucas came in with them. "Where did you come from?"

"Momma had to work the overnight shift, they called her in. Sandy said it would be all right if I stayed here last night."

"I didn't think you'd care, daddy."

"No, it's fine. Lucas is always welcome here. It's probably good you're here because I need to talk to all three of you."

"Did we do something wrong?" Sandy wanted to know.

"No, I wanted to ask you how y'all would feel if I asked Sarah to marry me."

The three children look from one to the other, Lucas was the first to speak. "Would that make you, my daddy?"

"If you would like that, I would be very happy to be your father."

"Would Lucas be my brother?" Colton asked.

"Yes, we would be all one big family."

"I vote for it."

"Will I have to call Sarah, momma?"

"Only if you want to, Sandy."

"Do you love her, daddy?"

"I do, very much."

"Then I think it's a great idea."

"Me too." Colton agreed again. "She never burns anything."

Jackson turned to Lucas, "how about you?"

"I want momma to be happy and I never really had a father, my daddy died before I could remember him. I think I like the idea of getting a father and a brother, and a sister all at one time. Sandy laughed. When are we all getting married?"

"As soon as I can convince your momma to marry me."

Lucas smiled, "Let's go ask her."

~~~

Jackson and Sarah decided to get married in two weeks on May 12. It was to be a small wedding at St. Mary's Lutheran Church. Sarah made sure that all of the children were involved in the planning. She had Sandy picked out the decorations in whatever color she preferred. Sandy picked ribbons of white and yellow to decorate the pews in the church. She wanted the flower arrangements in white, yellow, pink, and blue. Two were white, yellow and pink, the other two white, yellow and blue.

Sarah's flowers were white, pink and blue. Sandy said that pink was for Sarah, and the blue for her daddy. Sarah and Sandy picked out a beautiful floor-length dress in pale yellow for her. It was trimmed in pink and blue for both her daddy and Sarah. The boys wore blue suits with Colton wearing a blue tie for his daddy, and Lucas's wearing a pink tie for his momma. Sandy had come up with the idea.

The children stood next to their parents while they were united in marriage. The church was filled to capacity with well-wishers. In the back of the church a woman sat with a large hat pulled down. She had a pistol in her purse. Lisa wanted to kill both Jackson and Sarah, but came to her senses in time, there were too many witnesses around. Her arm still hurt, she wanted to strangle Sandy. "Another time." She said under her breath.

The reception was to be in the church's auditorium where a lot of the town functions were held. The entire wedding consisted of 30 people. To everyone's surprise many of the townspeople came.

Jackson pulled the Rev. Gerald Johnson aside before the ceremony. "I don't know where, or how you're going to do this, but I want to get enough food for everyone in the church. I'm good for the payment.
~~~

The Reverend looked around his church and called several of his parishioners up to talk to them. He explained the situation and asked them to help.

George Alexander said, "I'll go to my restaurant and open it up, announce that everyone should meet there. I'll make the Doc and Sarah the best wedding ever seen around these parts. Give me about an hour, I'll get my boys to help.

George Alexander had nine sons ranging from age 10 to 20 years old. Every one of them helped in the restaurant at one time. They all gathered to start the cooking. George had taken the wedding cake and personally transported it to his restaurant where he had his son, Leonard, set up a table for the cake.

After the ceremony was concluded, everyone was invited to George's restaurant for dinner. George and his sons set up a buffet for everyone. They got paper wedding plates with small silver bells across them, matching napkins, and silver forks and knives.

Jackson wondered where they got everything so fast, he turned to Sarah, "how did they do this in an hour?"

"Mr. Sanchez opened his variety store and took all of the supplies he had on hand. Miss Mabel gathered a variety of chocolates from her sweetshop and placed them in the center on all of the tables. The candles on the tables came from Miss Elaine's candle shop. The flowers from Miss Regena's flower shop."

"That's amazing."

"No, that's small town. They just opened up their stores and got what was needed."

The party lasted into the night. Jackson went to each person and thank them for everything they did. When it came time to go home, they couldn't find Colton.

"He wouldn't have left the building."

"Don't worry we'll find him, Jackson."

"Colton." Sarah called.

They looked for about 10 minutes before Lucas yelled from across the room. "I found him, Doc." He was standing next to a table holding the tablecloth up. He pointed, "he's under there."

Colton was sleepy and there were so many people around he didn't know where to go. He wandered over to the back of the restaurant and to a corner of the room, there was no one around him so he crawled underneath the table, made himself comfortable with the discarded towel and fell asleep.

Jackson pulled Colton out from under the table and into his arms. "I guess the parties over. This one is done in."

When they got home, Jackson carried Colton upstairs, undressed him, and rolled him into bed. He covered him, kissed him good night and left.

Lucas went directly to the bedroom he always used when he stayed over with them. He decided that it belonged to him now. Sandy and Stormy went to her bedroom. Sarah helped her out of her dress.

"Did you have fun?"

"It was great. I've never been to such a big party. Are you going to live with us forever now?"

Sarah laughed "that's the idea."

"Good. Daddy would never get that attic done alone, and I'm really tired of eating burned food."

After all the kids were tucked in bed, Jackson and Sarah fell into the couch down in the TV room. He put his arm around her and pulled her close. "Great wedding. Maybe we can do it again in about 20 years."

Chapter 24

When Paul answered his cell phone the last person, he expected it to be was Amanda. "Where are you?"

"Before I tell you, I think we need to talk a little."

"Let's start with I didn't shoot you. That wacko, Stanley Richards did. Alvin killed him."

"I saw who shot me, and I know it wasn't you."

"Listen, we need to get together, put all of this behind us. We can still make a life together, me, you, and the kid. I've got money, we will have money, lots of it."

"I don't know if I can trust you."

"That works both ways, let's meet."

"I'm staying with a friend. You know a drugstore in town called Coopers?"

"No, but I'll find it."

Paul spotted Amanda immediately, she was in the back by the soda fountain. He walked quickly over to her, "hey, Amanda. Have you changed the color of your hair? It seems a lot shorter also."

"Paul, sit down. Hey, kid, give this guy a chocolate soda."

Timmy looked over at Amanda and Paul, he didn't like how they looked, in fact he wanted to run. He knew they were up to something, but what? "Right away."

When he placed the soda in front of Paul, he noticed a tattoo on his hand, it looked like some kind of a devil. Paul again told

Amanda that he had a lot of money and he wanted to share it with her.

Lisa was waiting outside of the elementary school for Samantha and Colton to come out. She was hidden in a bush across from the school yard. In her crazed mind she decided if she got rid of the kids, and then Jackson's wife, he would come running back to her. She was going to start with Sandy and Colton.

"You will be right where you belong, dead. Jackson and I will have fun in Atlanta, together, just the two of us."

She had a 22 pistol she bought two years ago tucked in her pocket. She checked it for the fourth time to make sure that it was loaded. Next to her, laying on the ground, she had a grenade, a little something to assure that she would get away scott free. She planned on throwing it in the confusion, and then disappearing. The plan was perfect.

Lisa never considered that she would probably hurt others if she used the grenade. She couldn't see past her hate for the people who would mean the most to Jackson. After she killed Sandy and Colton, she would go after Sarah. She would go directly over to Jefferson Memorial and wait for her. She stuck her hand in the pocket and felt the bullet that was in there. This was a bullet she was saving just for Sarah.

Lisa looked at her watch for the sixth time. It was 9:55 A.M., just a few more minutes and her whole life would be exactly as she wanted it. She would have Jackson all to herself. When she got rid of the two kids, and Sarah, Jackson was free to marry her. They would be part of Atlanta's society, parties every night, socials, teas, and nothing but fun, fun, fun.

She looked up when she heard the bell ring, and then got into position, the waiting was over.

Lisa watched the kids burst out of the door and into the schoolyard. To her it sounded like a herd of elephants all honking at once. They headed for the swings and the jungle gym sets. She continued to watch, she didn't have to wait long. Sandy came out with another kid she didn't think she knew, she thought maybe it was that Lucas kid. They stopped next to the steps; they were waiting for Colton. She could wait a few more minutes.

When Lisa saw Colton come out of the door, she aimed directly at him. She fired and watched the boy drop. She continued to fire, but missed Sandy and hit the girl next to her who fell to the ground, nine-year-old Sally Kilmer.

Lucas ducked down and pulled Sandy down next to him, he glanced over to where the shots were fired. He yelled, "stay down."

"Colton?"

"I'll get him. Stay here."

He went down the two steps and dragged the young girl who had been shot over to the door. He looked into her face and knew that she was dead. Her eyes stared up into nothing. "Oh, God."

Children were running and screaming in every direction. Some went back into the building, but others ran wildly in every direction. Lisa was firing in all directions, then she picked up the grenade and threw it. Most of the children had scattered and were gone when the explosion went off. Two teachers Mr. Perry, and Miss Evans, who were playground monitors, and three other children were lying on the ground. Little six-year-old Sally Kilmer lay dead next to Lucas.

Another shot rang out and hit the brick wall right above Lucas's head. He flattened himself over Colton and pulled Sandy even closer. More shots were fired and all of them seemed to be aimed in their direction. In the distance he could hear a siren. Lisa also heard the siren, got up and ran.

Sandy lay flat on her belly and stared wide-eyed at Sally.

Lucas stripped off his jacket and pressed it against Colton's leg "don't look at her. There's nothing we can do for her. We have to help Colton."

Lucas looked over at the rest of the injured, there was nothing he could do to help them. Mr. Warren, the math teacher bent down to Colton. The little boy was crying. "I called the Sheriff; help is on the way."

"I've got this." Lucas said. "Go help the others."

Colton groaned and then screamed, "it hurts Lucas......."

"I know." Lucas bent down and spoke softly into Colton's ear. "I know it hurts; I know it hurts terrible, but you have to be still or you'll keep bleeding. We're going to get help. They're coming already, can't you hear the ambulance siren?"

Colton started to shake uncontrollably. "My leg." He moaned.

Lucas put his hand over Colton's eyes. "Close your eyes. Don't look. It's not too bad, but don't look."

The first ambulance arrived right after the Sheriff's Department. Paramedic Michael Donaldson went directly to Colton. He started to work on him immediately. He glanced at the other two children, "are either of you hurt?"

Sandy looked down at her shirt, it was covered with blood. "We're okay. Please, help my brother." She cried.

"Don't worry, honey. I'll take good care of him."

Paramedic Donaldson called into Jefferson Memorial. Jackson was in the emergency room and answered the call.

"We have a boy around seven..........."

"He's six." Sandy said.

"Six-year-old gunshot wound to the upper left leg. Bleeding is controlled, blood pressure 110/70, pulse 120. He's in a lot of pain."

"Administer D5W TKO, and give him an injection of morphine into the IV. Immobilize and transport immediately. Any change, call."

"Were be on our way, Doctor Shepard."

Neither Jackson Shepard or Michael Donaldson realized the child they were treating was Dr. Shepard son, Colton.

"Mike, how many more patients?"

"Maybe five. I'm not sure, Doc. I'm going to bring this little one in."

"Let me know if there's any changes."

"Will do."

Michael glanced over at Sally and quickly went to check her. She was deceased. He called back to Jefferson Memorial.

"Doc, I have a six or seven-year-old girl, gunshot wound to the chest. DOA. Poor kid never had a chance."

"Bring her in."

"The Sheriff's Department will take care of it. Ten-four." Mike looked at Sandy and Lucas. "Y'all go wait by the ambulance with your brother." Mike called the Sheriff over and explained about Sally. The Sheriff got a blanket and covered the child.

Mike hurried back to the ambulance and lightly ran his hand down his cheek. "You'll be fine."

"Call daddy." He whispered tears streaming down his cheek.

"We can call your daddy when we get to the hospital. Don't worry, baby, were going to make sure you get a nice ride over Jefferson Memorial. Can you tell me your name?"

"Colton Shepard."

"Your daddy Jackson Shepard?"

Colton shook his head. Sandy and Lucas piled into the front of the ambulance and rode with the driver, Tony Bookman, to the hospital.

When Mike rolled Colton into the emergency room, he asked for Dr. Shepard. Jackson was surprised when he saw his son on the gurney. He leaned down to reassure him and said, "just relax, son, and let me evaluated what's going on."

"It doesn't hurt too much now, daddy."

"Close your eyes, I'll be right here."

"Can I go home?"

"You need to have a few tests done and have to stay in the hospital overnight."

"I don't want to."

"I know you don't want to, but right now you have to go downstairs to take some pictures and make sure your leg is all right."

Colton yawned. The pain medication was starting to take effect and Jackson will could see him visibly relax. He looked over at Mike, "where are my other children?"

"Sandy and Lucas are fine. I've got them stashed in the waiting room."

Sarah came running into the room and went directly over to Colton. She took his hand and kissed his forehead. "How do you feel?"

"I'm okay, Sarah, daddy gave me some medicine so it doesn't hurt so bad."

"Sarah, stay with Colton. I had to check on Sandy and Lucas."

"They're in chairs. I spoke to them; besides being shaken they seem to be all right. Lucas tried to help a little girl that died."

"Stay with Colton, I'll be right back."

Jackson made sure he wasn't needed for the other emergencies that flooded in before he went to find his children.

Lucas was sitting next to Sandy with his arm around her and she was leaning into him. He went to them, bent down and asked, "are you two, okay? Neither one of you were hurt?"

"Were fine, Doc."

Sandy threw herself into Jackson's arms. He picked her up and told Lucas to follow him. He took them to the quiet of the doctor's lounge. Sandy had curled up into his lap.

"My shirt, daddy, it's all covered in blood. I need to get it off. I want it off."

Jackson put her in the chair. "I'll be right back."

He came back with a small set of scrubs for Sandy and Lucas. He pointed to a doorway, "the showers are back there."

Once they were showered and changed, they both felt much better. Sandy went over to Jackson and crawled back into his lap. He wrapped his arms around her and gently squeezed.

"Lucas, are you alright? Mike said you tried to help a little girl who died."

"Sally, I knew her. I tried, but it was too late and I couldn't help her."

"The important thing is that you tried."

"Daddy." Sandy shuttered. "I saw who shot everyone."

"Are you sure?"

"I'm as sure as I am looking at you."

"We'll have to go and tell the Sheriff."

"It was Lisa."

Lisa? Are you absolutely sure?"

"Yes, I saw her, she looked right at me and then ran away."

Chapter 25

Jackson wanted to keep it quiet that his daughter saw Lisa and identified her as the shooter. He asked the Sheriff to join them in the doctor's lounge. Sandy and Lucas had crammed themselves together into a chair. Jackson took a deep breath and tried to control his anger.

"Sandy, you have to tell Sheriff Dustin what you just told me."

Sandy looked over at the Sheriff, but went directly over to her father. "Are you mad at me, daddy?"

Jackson softened immediately, he smiled at his little girl and hugged her. "No, not at you. I just want you to tell the Sheriff what you saw and say it in your own words."

Lucas took Sandy's hand and urged her to tell the Sheriff what she had just told him. "It's okay. I won't let everything happen to you." He said bravely.

Sandy turned the Sheriff. "I saw Lisa Fredericks there. She shot at us and then threw something that made a loud noise and everyone fell down."

The Sheriff shook his head, "a grenade was thrown. Are you sure that you saw Lisa Fredericks?"

"Yes sir, I'm positive, and then she ran over to Berry Valley Street."

"Most of the gunshots were aimed at us." Lucas said. "I saw the flash from the gun and a lot of them hit the building behind me."

"Did you see Lisa Fredericks too?"

"No. I was kinda busy. Doc, where's Colton? Is he alright?"

"The bullet hit him in the upper thigh, but he'll be okay. He has to stay in the hospital for a few days because I want to put him on antibiotic IV therapy so he doesn't get an infection."

"Daddy, he can't stay without Norman. We have to bring Norman to him."

"Who is Norman?" The Sheriff wanted to know.

"Norman is Colton's teddy bear."

"Oh, all right. Doc, do you know where I can find this Lisa Fredericks?"

Jackson gave the Sheriff all the information he knew about Lisa and where she might be found. They were all tired and wanted to go home, so he asked if the rest of this questioning could wait until tomorrow.

Colton had his leg x-rayed and then was sent to have a CAT scan. Jackson and Sarah decided that she would go home with Sandy and Lucas and he would stay at the hospital with Colton.

Colton would be in the hospital for four days. When he came home, they decided to have a little party for him. Sarah made a cake. They all watched a movie in the TV room and Jackson ordered pizza. Later he made popcorn for everyone.

Colton was placed in the big recliner and Sarah propped up his leg up to make him more comfortable. Stormy lay on the end of the recliner next to Colton.

The Twilight Zone doorbell rang. Jackson got up to answer it. "Daddy, we have to change that doorbell." Sandy called to him as he left the room.

He was surprised to find the Sheriff on his doorstep.

"Hey, Johnny, come on in."

Thank you, Doc. I need to talk to you and Sarah, in private."

"Fine, let's go into the kitchen. I'll go get Sarah."

Jackson went back to the TV room. "You kids watch the movie while Sarah and I go speak to the Sheriff. Lucas, watch Colton and if there's a problem come and get me."

Sarah made coffee and sat down across from the Sheriff. "I'm sorry to disturb y'all at home, but I wanted to tell you before this gets out into the newspapers.

"What's wrong, Johnny?"

"Well, Doc, Lisa Franklin is dead."

Nothing could have surprised Jackson more. "What? How?"

"We found her at her aunt's home, she made it very clear she wasn't going to come willingly and pulled a gun on us. We tried to get her to drop it, but she wouldn't. I talked to her for over an hour, and got nothing, then she tried to shoot Rance. I had to shoot her."

"I'm sorry, Johnny. I'm sorry that Lisa is dead, even sorrier that you had to be the one to kill her."

"She had good reason not to want to be arrested. We found her aunt, in her bedroom, and very dead. She had been dead for a long time. We found her when we searched the house. Lisa killed her. The woman had two bullet holes in her chest. I believe she was shot right there in her own bed, and by the time we found her she was almost skeletal, so it was a long time ago. Lisa must've put her in there. The covers were pulled up to her chin and it was like she was sleeping, there was a chair pulled up to the bed and open book next to it. Lisa was reading to her every night.

Lisa must've been staying with her because the other bedroom had been obviously occupied by her. Doc, there are all kinds of pictures on the wall. They were plastered everywhere."

"Pictures of what?" Sarah asked.

The Sheriff pointed at Jackson. "The pictures were of Jackson. There had to be hundreds of them. You and your kids. There were even a few of Sarah."

Jackson leaned back in the chair and let out a low whistle "I don't even know what to say to that."

"She also left a diary, a lot of it was rambling, mostly about you. How she loved you. How you had to be hers. How she couldn't live without you. How you were always meant to be together. That you and she were soulmates. She had a plan to make sure that the two of you would be back together forever, and that nothing would ever keep you apart again."

"I never realized." Jackson shook his head. "She had to be mentally ill, delusional, but she hid it well."

"It's worse than you thought. She shot your boy, and killed little Nancy, but I don't think Nancy was the target. The real target was your children. She also shot the rest of the people over at the school. Oh, and the pictures of your children and Sarah, they were blocked out in black ink and then slashed with a knife. She meant business and would've killed all of them. She also cut Sarah's brakes on her car.

Sarah gasped. "Oh, my God, how could she do all this?"

"She's also broke into your home, Doc. She wrote how she was waiting in the attic and tried to scare Sandy. She wanted to make it so frightening to live here that you would run back to Atlanta, and to her. She was going to kill Sandy that night the dog found her and made the ruckus. It's better this way, she had been taken in she would've been put into a mental institution, and if she was released someday, she would be after you again. They don't change. One more thing, and I hate to tell you this, but she killed your wife. It was all there in the diary. She was so desperate to have you she had to kill her best friend."

Jackson shook his head slowly, "Mary. My poor Mary, she didn't deserve that."

Sarah put her arms around Jackson. "It's not your fault. You didn't know."

"I never suspected her, never suspected that she would do something like that."

"Sorry, Doc, but I felt that you needed to know this. Your wife's death will no longer be a cold case."

"Somehow that doesn't make me feel any better."

After the sheriff left, Jackson and Sarah decided they had to tell the children about Lisa. They would tell them not only of her death, but of her trying to scare Sandy. Jackson would not tell the children that she killed their mother.

"So, it wasn't a bad dream. She was my ghost all along?" Asked Sandy.

"She was the ghost, but she will never be able to scare you again."

"I'm sorry she had to die, daddy. I don't understand why she did all that."

"Lisa was sick, mentally sick. She wasn't thinking right."

Chapter 26

Paul had finally convinced Amanda to live with him, again. The first thing she did was find them a new apartment that was closer to Lone Mountain, it was in a small area called, Topeka. It was approximately 25 miles away and wasn't much more than a truck stop just off of the interstate.

It was a large gas stop for truckers that were going north. It was made up of a combination store and lunch counter that actually serve breakfast, lunch, and dinner. They closed dinner down at 8 PM, and if someone was hungry there were sandwiches and coffee available. There were also showers in the back if the truckers stopped overnight. There was a small makeshift motel, or they could sleep in their trucks if they had cabs.

The truck stop was called, Mick's. Behind Mick's was a large area where the truckers would lay up overnight, and directly across from that was a small resident area where the workers had apartments. Currently there were four of the six apartments being used. Times were not the best in this business and getting help was difficult.

Amanda had taken a job at Mick's so she could get the free housing. Paul and Alvin immediately moved in with her. The residence was supposed to house only the workers, but there was little supervision at the apartment complex, and Amanda claimed they were her boyfriends and were staying for that one night. No one would question it. The other three residents there kept to themselves because they were doing the exact same thing.

Manuel Torres was an illegal who had his wife, Carmen, and two children, Pete and Joe living with him. Pete and Joe were really named Pedro and Jesus, but Manual felt they would fit in better if they had American names. Carmen was also working for Mick's; she did the daily cleanup while Manuel worked the night shift. Amanda very seldom saw the children. They wanted to stay under the radar and never caused any trouble.

The second apartment was occupied by a black man who did what little maintenance he could to keep his apartment status. He spent a lot of his time with the bottle. His name was Bruce Sequim. He was originally from Michigan where he left 25 years ago and cut off all ties with his family and friends. He was an alcoholic with an arrest warrant for murdering his best friend, Earl Langerin, in a bar fight. He would be arrested a month later.

In Michigan, Earl was known as Bob James. He always claimed that the death of his friend was an accident. He was so riddled with guilt that he drank to forget.

The last occupied apartment was an elderly woman. She worked the morning shift, and Amanda worked the afternoon shift. They would briefly encounter each other when they exchange places. Ellen Tasker was 68 years old, and blamed everyone but herself for her crappy life. She hated everyone, and everything, was gruff with the customers, sometimes did no more than snap one-word answers to them.

Amanda started to work at two in the afternoon. She always made sure she was presentable, had a smile on her face, and was pleasant and friendly to all the truckers. Sometimes it got her good tips. She had no intentions of staying in the situation the rest of her life. She was using Paul until she could get out.

Paul and Alvin would disappear for days and always come back with a substantial amount of money. She never asked where they got it. She was carefully putting away as much money as she could, and since she didn't trust either Paul or Alvin, so she buried the money in a glass jar on the other side of the apartment complex. There was a small grass and tree area between the freeway and the apartment building and she found the perfect place where the money would remain undetected. It was her private escape plan. She may have to bolt one day and she would need a lot of money.

Amanda never thought about the baby that she left behind. She was no longer Mandy Sterling, but Amanda Dean. She liked her job and there was no place for a kid, much less a sick one. She didn't really care what happened to him, so she just put him out of her mind. In her opinion he was better off, and so was she.

"Hey there, Amanda."

Amanda was stocking shelves, she turned and smiled at Pat Dickerson, he was a long-haul trucker. He came through once a week. He usually stayed from Friday night to Monday morning and then came back the following Friday. It had become a pattern. She liked him and thought he felt the same about her.

She gave him a bright smile. "Good morning, Pat. Are you getting ready to take off for the week?"

"I am, but I'll be back on Friday so I was thinking you and me could go off to Atlanta and have some fun."

Amanda wanted nothing more than to have fun, and it was time that she had some. She jumped at the chance to go to Atlanta. "I'll be waiting for you to return, it's a date."

Amanda loved to go places and have fun. Even when she lived with her momma and daddy, and that brat brother of hers all she wanted to do was have fun. Her parents were so strict she wasn't allowed to go out of the house without them, and they rarely left the house.

On the few occasions when she got up the courage to sneak out, they always found out somehow, and she was punished severely.

Her mother would lock her in her room for weeks at a time. She could see no one, talk to no one, and basically do nothing. During this time, they didn't talk to her or interact in any way.

Her mother, Alice Jean striped her bedroom of everything including the bed. She had only a blanket to sleep on and every morning her mother would come in and drop a dress on the floor. No underwear, just a plain gray dress, and she never said a word to her. They had nailed shut the windows in her bedroom so she couldn't escape.

All she was allowed to do was sit and do nothing every day, day after day. She sat in the empty room waiting for the sun to go down and then the door opened again. A tray was shoved in, the door was slammed and locked.

Amanda had tried three times to get out. The first time it was just to have fun, but the last two times were for her to leave for good. They always were one step ahead of her, she was caught and it was back to isolation.

"Just one more damn secret that house kept."

~~~

Paul, Alvin, and Amanda were sitting around the kitchen table. Paul looked over at her and said again, "you know that house better than I do, and Alvin has never been in it."

"I don't want to go back there."

"Why? The money and jewelry are in that house. I put them there."
~~~

"Let it go. That house has so many secrets that this will just be another one."

"What kind of secrets?"

"Just secrets. Secrets left better not know. I can't go back there."

Alvin jumped up and grabbed Amanda. He screamed, "you'll do it. There's a lot of money at stake here. We'll be set for a very long time."

"Let her go, Alvin."

Amanda punched him in the chest. Paul yelled, "stop it. The matter is settled and we're going to go get the money."

"How? You said it wasn't there when you went back."

"Someone in that house knows where the money and jewels are, all we have to do is get one of them to talk."

"Who lives there?" Amanda wanted to know.

"Some doctor, his wife and three kids. I've been watching them for some time now. That youngest kid was involved in that school shooting a couple weeks ago. He's at home now because he got shot."

"Who would shoot a kid?" Amanda asked.

Alvin snorted. "Lots of people would. Kids are a pain in the ass."

"I've got an idea. This woman in the paper, Lisa someone, the story is that she tried to scare the kids of the house. The kid.... Alvin, get the paper."

Paul search through the paper for the story. He found it and also found Sandy's name. "Yeah, Sandy, she's the one who believes there is a ghost in the house." He put the paper down. "Maybe we can make her believe the ghost is still there."

"Then what?" Alvin said.

"If we can scare this kid bad enough, daddy will want to get her out of there. When they're gone, we can pull that house apart if we want to. If that doesn't work, we can snatch the kid and force her to talk."

"What if she doesn't know anything?"

"Someone knows and if we have the kid, they'll tell us. First, I want to see if we can scare them out."

Chapter 27

"Hurry it up, Colton." Sandy called up the stairway. "Daddy's going to drive us."

"I'm hurrying, my leg won't hurry." He said as he slowly descended the stairs.

"Daddy said you're all better, so move it."

"Okay, okay I'm coming."

"Come on, bro." Lucas laughed.

Jackson dropped the three kids off at school and went on to the hospital. Sarah was off today and decided to tackle the kitchen. She had a productive morning, cleaning and rearranging. She stopped for lunch and heard the Twilight Zone doorbell go off."

"Sandy's right, we have to change that."

When she went to answer the door, no one was there. She looked down the hill but saw no one. The house sits alone on the top of a large hill with the nearest neighbor at the end of the road and to the left. There were all kinds of houses that were tucked in the forest area that they lived in, but there were large separations between them and it made the area very private.

Sarah looked around but everything seemed quiet, she looked down at Stormy who plopped herself down to wait. "Come on, Stormy let's get back to our project."

Amanda quickly moved through the kitchen and up the stairs to the second floor she went to the fifth bedroom on the left and slipped inside. She went directly to the closet, felt along the floor and pressed a button that popped the door open to reveal a stair case above. She ducked so she wouldn't hit her head on a low beam, and pressed a button on the other side that snapped the door closed.

Amanda and her brother, Bobby Joe had found this passageway when they were very little. It took them up to yet another side of the vast attic that had been closed off by a wall partition. You couldn't tell from either side that the attic extended further. This side of the attic had just as much furniture as the other side did, lamps, bookcases with books still in them, and clocks. All kinds of clocks. The area was filled from front to back with a variety of everything imaginable.

She lightly touched a large Rocking Horse she had as a child. She ran her hand through its mane, she had loved this Rocking Horse so much. Bobby Joe was jealous and demanded something better than her Rocking Horse, so her father bought him a full-size horse. That horse was now in Colton's bedroom, the horse that he called Buck.

Amanda sat down in a chair across from her Rocking Horse and stared at it. "It was always him. Always what Bobby Joe wanted, he got anything and everything and it had to be bigger and better.

In the end she had gotten revenge. I surely did, my little Rocking Horse. I knew that he was the one who told on me all of those times, those rotten times when they locked me up. Nothing! I had nothing, but I got even with the little Bastard. I got even with all of them.

"Only the house knows what I did. The house, and now you will know because I'm going to tell you everything that happened. I remember that night, it was dark, windy, and moonless. It had threatened rain all day. Mother and father had spent the entire day arguing and screaming at each other. My brother, Bobby Joe, spent his time tormenting me."

"Go away, brat."

"I can't, just listen to them down there."

Amanda put down the book she was reading and listened. "This is the worst that they've ever been."

There was a large crash from downstairs. "The clock in the hall." Bobby Joe laughed. "I never did like that old clock."

"You're horrid. I hate it when they fight like this."

"So go to your bedroom. Do you enjoy being in there now that momma has stripped it and there's nothing left? "

Amanda got up and pushed Bobby Joe. "Get away from me, you lousy little brat."

Billy Joe's anger bristled and he spat at her, "I'm telling momma. She'll lock you up in there for a month."

"You open your trap; Bobby Joe and I'll make you regret it."

There was another crash from downstairs. "What do you think that was?" Asked Bobby Joe. "It sounds to me like that ugly purple lamp momma loved so much."

"Bobby Joe, get yourself down here, right now!" Alice Jean screamed from the stairway.

"Wow, she sounds pissed off. Y'all better hurry on, Bobby Joe."

"Go suck a lemon."

Amanda turned back to the Rocking Horse, "you see how he was? Always a nasty child. Momma packed herself up, and then she got Bobby Joe packed up. She said she was going off with him so daddy couldn't ever see him again. She was screaming about how she was going to get a divorce and keep Bobby Joe all to herself. As she left, she yelled to daddy that he would never see his son again."

Amanda got up and paced the entire attic, she did this three times and then came back and stood directly in front of the Rocking Horse. "She didn't want me. Never even looked my way as she rushed Bobby Joe out of the door. Just like that, never even a goodbye. Momma was always a bitch to me, but I fixed everything and I'm going to tell you exactly how, or maybe you already know because you've been in the house all this time."

Amanda sighed deeply and sat down across from the Rocking Horse again. "I did it. I did it all. I killed momma, daddy, he was the hardest, and Bobby Joe.

I started by following them. When she slammed out the door, she went over to the motel on 51, the one right near the big Lake. I waited until night because I knew the minute momma fell asleep Bobby Joe would sneak out." She whispered like someone might hear her. "He did drugs, started with marijuana and went to cocaine. The little snot. If I had let him live, he probably would've acquired at least a $500 a day habit.

I watched them come out of the motel and followed him over to the lake where he met up with Toby Candles. That's his drug connection. I watched as Bobby Joe handed over a lot of money to Toby, and I wondered where he got it. I never did find that out. Anyhow, Rocking Horse, I waited until his back was turned to me and Toby had left, and then I killed him. I did it right there by the lake and just left his body."

Amanda stopped talking when she heard a loud bang from downstairs. She waited until it became quiet again. She got up and moved closer to the Rocking Horse. She lowered her voice, "where were we? Oh, yes, after I killed Bobby Joe, I didn't know what to do with him so that's why I left him right there by the lake. Then, I went back to the motel. Bobby Joe had left the door open so I went in very quietly.

Momma looked almost normal lying there, like she might've actually been a nice person, but I knew better. I smothered her with a pillow. It was easier than I thought it would be. After I was sure she was dead, I went back to the house to get daddy's car so I could take her somewhere. I didn't really know where I was going to take her, but I couldn't carry her so I needed the car. Daddy was so drunk that I could have driven the car right through the house and he would've never woken up. I took the car and went back to get momma. It was a good thing that she was smaller than me because even being little she was heavy.

I sat in the car for a long time trying to think where I should take her and then it came to me. I drove her to the forest preserve on Kerry Mountain. There was a blanket in the back of the car so I put her on it and dragged her deep into the forest until I found the perfect spot." Amanda laughed. "It must be the perfect spot. When I came home, I knew I had to do something about daddy. Daddy, daddy, daddy. I really didn't want to kill him, but there was no choice at that point.

I half dragged and half walked daddy over to the upstairs railing. I sat him down on the carpet and went to get a rope. He was snoring when I put it around his neck. I woke him up just enough so that he could stumble toward the railing for me. I tied one end of the rope to the banister so all I had to do was give him a little push.

Daddy died real fast, and then I left and disappeared, and now I'm back."

Chapter 28

Amanda thought Paul's plan was crazy, but she had to do it. In a lot of aways she was still afraid of him and when he insisted on something she didn't argue with him. She waited until it was after one in the morning before she went downstairs. She cautiously opened the bedroom door and found a little boy sleeping in the bed. The next bedroom she found Sandy.

This was her target. It was now time to go into action. She had to make this kid believe she was dead and had come to haunt her. Paul wanted her to continue the whole ghost thing. She had prepared herself before she came.

Amanda spent several hours putting on makeup and dressing for the part. She looked like she had just stepped out of a grave. She went into the bedroom, over to the bed and waved a sheer handkerchief across Sandy's face. She stirred and turned over.

Amanda leaned down and whispered into her ear, "Sandy............... Look at me. I have come to talk to you. I have come a long way. All the way from the grave."

Sandy wasn't quite awake as she sat up in the bed. At first, she didn't see anyone so she called out, "who's there?"

"Amanda slapped her hand over Sandy's mouth, smiled and whispered loudly into her ear, "I am the secret in this house, and you also have a secret one that we have to share. Where did you hide the money?"

"Money? What are you...............? go away." She yelled and tried to strike out.

Amanda pushed Sandy down on the bed and got right in her face, "I'll be back for the money and the jewelry that you have, it belongs to the house and we wanted back, so you better come up with it or you die."

Sandy was so frightened she could hardly move. Amanda retreated slowly out of the door and disappeared. Sandy screamed and continued to scream. When Jackson came over to the bed and put his arms around her, she started to fight with him. "Get away. Get away. I don't know what you want, go away."

"Sandy. Sandy it's daddy."

"Daddy, daddy is that you really you?"

"You're having a bad dream."

"No, I saw the ghost again and this time it wasn't Lisa. I don't know who it was, but she said she would hurt me, kill me if I didn't tell her where the money is. I don't know about any money. I don't want to stay here."

Jackson slowly rocked Sandy as he held her tightly against him. "There's no one here. It was just a bad dream."

"Well, if it's just a dream it sure was a real enough. The ghost whispered in my ear and said she'd be back."

~~~

Amanda slammed the door when she went into the apartment. Alvin ran to her, "did you get the money? The jewelry?"

"Back off Alvin. Where's Paul?"

"In the bedroom, I'll go get him."

Paul grabbed Amanda and kissed her. "Hey, baby."
~~~

"Don't you, hey, baby me. I told you this was a stupid idea. Even if I could scare the kid, I sure wouldn't scare that big ass father of hers, who almost caught me. You moron, you sent me to the house were my doctor lives." She hit him in the chest, "that's the doctor who took care of me at Jefferson Memorial. The doctor who knows me, the doctor who delivered my kid, and if he got a good look at me, he would know exactly who I am. I told you it was a stupid plan and that it wouldn't work, but no, you insisted I had to go there."

"I didn't know that was the doctor who treated you, how could I?"

She pointed her finger at them, "the both of you just shut the hell up, and stop arguing with me."

"All right Amanda, where's the jewelry and money?"

"I didn't get it. I don't know where it is. Do you have any idea how big that freaking house is? It could be anywhere in there. Paul, you said it was in the attic, is that right?"

"Yes, last time I saw the money it was in the attic."

"Well, genius, do you know that there are two attics in that house? There are partitioned off from each other and one of them has your secret. I don't believe anybody knows about it except me."

"Well then it probably isn't in the attic anymore. Didn't you get anything out of the kid?"

"There wasn't time."

"You'll have to go back."

"Forget it. It won't work."

"Fine. Okay, then we go to Plan B."

"What exactly is Plan B, Paul?"

"We take the kid. If she doesn't know where the money and jewelry is someone else in that household does and will give it up to save her."

~~~

"I'm telling you that ghosts don't exist."

"Then, why do they keep bothering me?"

Lucas set his backpack down and turned to Sandy. "Doc said you had a bad dream and that's all it was."

"Well, this dream touched me and spoke to me. It wanted to know what I did with the money."

"What money?"

"How do I know."

Colton had been standing in the doorway, meekly he said "maybe I do."

"What does that mean?" Lucas asked.

"I got money. I got lots of money. I found it."

"Found it where?"

Colton pointed up at the ceiling. "Up there, in the attic."

"Show me."

They went up to the attic and Colton took them to the added room at the end where the four dolls sat with their tea party. Lucas looked at them and then turned to Colton. "I don't see any money, only dolls."

Sandy was examining the dolls. "They're really beautiful."
~~~

"There dolls." Lucas said absentmindedly. "Colton, where's the money?"

He pointed to the floor. "That's where it was, but I took it."

"That's why it's not here now, where did you take it?"

"Bucks guarding it."

"Buck? Your wooden horse?"

"I put it in the saddlebags."

"Let's go back downstairs."

Just as they walked into Colton's room, Sarah called, "breakfast."

"Lucas went over to the staircase and yelled down, "be right down."

He went back over to Colton's bedroom and pulled down the saddlebags from Buck's back. He unhooked them and found all of the money Colton said he took. There were stacks and stacks of bills all in hundreds. "You found this in the attic?"

"Sure did."

Sarah called up the stairs again, "kids, hurry it up."

Lucas shoved the money back into the saddlebags and placed it back over Buck's rump. He grinned, the horse almost looked real, like it would just take off running at any moment. Whoever had Buck before must've loved him just like Colton did now. He petted the horse's neck, "good job."

Colton pointed to the door. "We better go, Sarah called us for a third time."

"All right," Lucas agreed. "We'll tell mom and Doc about this tonight, right now we better hurry before momma has a fit."

When they got to school Colton didn't want to go in. He sat down on the steps and refused to move. Lucas sat down and pulled his little brother next to him. The bell already rang and they were all going to be late. He told Sandy to go ahead and they would be right along.

Lucas turned back to Colton, "why don't you want to go in?"

"It's Monday." He said like that would explain everything.

"Monday? What's wrong with Monday?"

"We have to go in front of the whole class and I don't want to."

"Why do you have to go in front of the whole class?"

"They make us talk about stuff."

"Talk about what?"

"Every Monday," Colton explained patiently, "we have to write a story about something and read it out loud in front of the entire class."

"Did you write a story?"

"Yeah." He pulled a crumpled paper out of his pocket and handed it to Lucas.

The paper was folded into six pieces. He unfolded it and smoothed it out. Lucas read the story that Colton had written, it was about a wild horse Park where all of the horses lived and could run free. No one could go there except for the horses, so they would always be safe. He wrote how one horse took care of all the others, that horse was his Buck.

"It's a good story. Why don't you want to read it?"

"I don't want to; they all look at you."

"You mean the other kids?"

"Yeah."

"Okay, Colton, here's what you do. You go up there, read your story and don't look at the other kids. Pretend you're reading it to Buck because it's really his story."

"How is it his story?"

"He's the hero in your story, so pretend you're telling it to him."

"But he's not there."

"You know Buck, you see him every day, so all you have to do is imagine he's in the back of the room standing there waiting for you to read this paper just to him."

"Do you think that will work?"

"Sure, it will, just don't look at all those other kids. Come on, were late."

When Lucas walked into his classroom the Dark Mistress of Doom, Mrs. Bertha Lytle was standing where his teacher, Mr. Tracy should've been. He looked at her and groaned.

"Can you explain why you are late?"

It took him five minutes to explain about Colton and the paper, but he didn't think that she wanted to understand. He was given detention, five days of staying after class, one hour each day and told to sit down.

Lucas shrugged, "fine."

She turned red, he thought she was about ready to bust, but all she did was tell him he should go sit down. When Lucas got to his seat he looked over to Sandy, but she wasn't there. He immediately looked around the entire room. He didn't see her anywhere in the classroom.

"Hey, Slick, he called to the boy across from him. "Where's Sandy?"

"She didn't come in, isn't she with you?"

"No."

Lucas threw his books down on the desk. He instantly knew that something was very wrong. Sandy would've gone directly to the classroom. Where was she?

"Mr. Lucas Carson!" Mrs. Lytle yelled. "Do plan on disrupting this whole class all day?"

"Where's my sister? Where is Savanna Shepard? She should be here."

"Evidently, young man, she isn't here."

"I have to leave."

"You cannot walk out of school."

"I have no choice. I have to find Sandy."

"You will not leave."

"Sorry." Lucas yelled and ran out the back classroom door. He heard the Mistress of Doom screaming after him, "come back here."

Lucas didn't stop until he was outside of school. He quickly backtracked to where they had been and found nothing. He had to call someone who would actually listen to him. He would call the hospital and asked for Dr. Shepard.

Jackson listened carefully to what Lucas was saying. "Do you have any idea where she would've gone?"

"No, I thought she went to class while I was talking to Colton. That was the last time I saw her. "

"Where are you now?"

"Just outside of the school, by the green door."

"You stay there, I'm going to call the Sheriff and then I'll be by to pick you and Colton up."

"We'll be right outside the green door."

All of the doors at the school were designated with colors, the red door had been painted red, the blue door, blue, the green door, green and so on. There were six doors with 6 different colors.

Lucas went back into the school and over to Colton's classroom. He went in and directly over to his brother. "Come with me. We have to hurry."

Colton got up and Lucas took his hand. The teacher stopped him at the door. "My daddy is waiting for us. He can explain everything later."

He ignored, Miss Hays, Colton's teacher and quickly walked out of the door with him. "We have to hurry."

Lucas sat down with Colton on the same steps they had been on earlier. Suddenly, he shook with fear, the fear he felt for Sandy.

Chapter 29

Paul had gone into the school earlier and broke into the janitor's closet. He slipped on a work shirt and took a toolbox. He went into the hall and wandered around until he spotted Sandy. She came in late and all the other kids were already in class, all the better for him. He silently came up behind her, put his hand over her mouth and nose so she couldn't scream. The chloroform worked quickly and she was unconscious in a minute. He carried her into the janitor's closet and then stuffed her into a cloth bag that he had brought with him. He slung her over his shoulder and walked out the back door, no one had seen him. He dumped the bag into the car trunk and slowly drove away.

Sandy groaned and turned over, she was extremely groggy and wasn't exactly sure what was going on. She looked around the room and didn't recognize anything. Her head was pounding and the light hurt her eyes. She closed them for a few minutes and tried to think.

The last thing that she remembered was walking into school. She was late because Colton didn't want to go in for some reason that she couldn't remember.

Sandy forced herself to get up, she took a few steps and stopped waiting for the dizziness that hit her to go away. She continued on to the door, but discovered that it was locked. Just as she was going to bang on the door, she stopped. It might not be the best thing to do and she might be better if she didn't make any noise at all. Someone took her and had brought her here, her only thoughts were that she needed to get away.

She went back to the bed and sat on the edge of it. She let her eyes roam around the room, there wasn't much in it. The bed, a small dresser, a lamp and an empty closet.

The door was locked, but there were two windows. She went over to each window and tried to open them; they wouldn't move. When she looked down at the window sill she knew why. The windows had been nailed shut. She looked out the window, but could see very little, mostly what she saw were trees.

Paul finished the note to Dr. Shepard and handed it to Amanda. "Just shove it into the mailbox and get the hell out of there."

Amanda threw the envelope back at Paul, "send Alvin. I don't want to go back there."

Paul stood over Amanda "now, what the hell's wrong with you?"

"I might be recognized by someone. Don't forget I lived in this town until I was 16. You shouldn't have taken that kid. I can't believe you did it at the school."

"Relax, no one saw me."

"That kid knows about the money." Alvin said. "I'm going in and finding out exactly where it is."

Paul grabbed Alvin by the arm. "Leave the kid alone."

"Why? What are we waiting for?"

"Let Shepard get the letter. Her old man is a doctor, so if they don't know where the money and jewelry is at, maybe we can get the money out of him."

"One of them took it. Who else could have? I'm betting on the Doc's little wife."

"It doesn't matter because either we get the jewelry store goods back, or the Doc pays a fee to get the kid back. Amanda go deliver it."

She grabbed the envelope, went to the door and slammed it. She called back at him, "I'll do it after dark."

When Amanda went back to the house, she found several the Sheriff's cars sitting outside. There was a lot of activity surrounding the entire house and she wasn't about to go to the mailbox to put in the stupid letter. She waited until she saw the Sheriff's deputy standing on the other side of the road. He was far away from the cars. She snuck up and threw the letter into the open window of the Sheriff's car and then quickly ran back to the wooded area.

Amanda felt like her heart was beating a thousand beats a minute. She didn't think she was this scared when she got shot. She was sure that no one had seen her and quietly as possible turned and went back through the trees and over to the road where she had left the car.

She didn't like the way everything was going. She didn't want to be involved with kidnapping a child. She didn't trust Paul or Alvin, especially Alvin. He was a hothead and unpredictable. Sometimes he scared her and she tried too never be alone with him. She had to get out and run as far away from them as she could. She had been a fool to think that Paul had changed. She knew deep in her gut that they were going to kill this kid, and maybe her too.

Amanda stopped the car along the road and leaned over the steering wheel, she had to think, but she was suddenly exhausted and found it a hard task.

~~~
~~~

Sheriff Dustin asked Lucas to tell him once again what happened at the school. They were interrupted by Deputy Longmen who handed him a letter.

"Where did you find this?"

"On the seat of the sheriff's car. We didn't see anyone, and we searched the surrounding area, but found nothing."

"Thanks, Rance."

Sheriff Dustin opened the envelope and slipped the letter into a plastic sleeve. He put it down on the table so that they all could read it.

The letter read:

Doc,

We got your daughter, Savannah, and you have my money. I want the money back all $180,000 of it.

NO COPS!

We don't want to hurt your little girl and right now she is fine. She will stay that way, but only if we get the money back. You will be contacted again. The kid for the $180,000.

DON'T SCREW IT UP!

You will be contacted.

The Sheriff turned to Jackson, "that's it. Doc, do you have any idea who could have sent this to you?"

"No, and I have no clue what he's even talking about."

Sarah picked up the letter and read it again. "I don't know who this could be either." She put the letter back down on the table. And called Lucas and Colton. "Let them read it and see if they recognize anything."

Lucas studied the letter for the third time and looked up at his mother, "Sorry. I don't know who wrote it."

"Me either, Sarah. Where's Sandy? Why can't she come home?"

"Were trying to bring her home, Colton." Jackson said and took him into his arms.

Colton looked deep into his father's eyes, "can't the Sheriff go get her?"

"He doesn't know where she is, but we'll find her. Lucas, would you take Colton upstairs and help him get into bed?"

"Sure. Come on, Colton."

"What do we do next Sheriff?" Sarah asked.

"We wait until the next letter comes, but in the meantime, we are all going to search for Sandy. Knock on doors, see if anyone has seen anything. There's a lot of nosy people in our town. I'll leave Deputy Nance here with you. Doc, call immediately if you get contacted. Sit tight."

From behind Jackson a little voice called, "daddy."

He turned around and looked at Colton, he had taken off his shirt and stood there in his jeans. Lucas was standing next to him holding his hand. In Colton's other arm was his soldier box. Lucas had the saddlebags draped over his shoulder.

"What is this?"

"It's money, daddy, and my soldiers are guarding the treasure."

"What treasure?"

Colton placed the box on the floor and opened the top. He took out all of his armies and gave the box to Jackson.

He looked down into the box and call the Sheriff over, "Johnny, look at this."

The Sheriff looked down into the box. "This might be that jewelry store heist that happened over in Marrow. The proprietor was killed. The store was cleaned out of all of the jewelry and $7000 in cash was also taken.

Lucas held up the saddlebags, "there's more in here."

"Where did you get this, Lucas?" Jackson asked.

"Colton actually found it, he said it was from upstairs in the attic. The main one."

"What do you mean, the main one?"

"There's another attic up there, Doc, and it's full just like the one we've been cleaning up. I found it in the back of the closet of that fifth bedroom nobody uses. It looks like somebody's been up there because the dust is kind of moved around."

"I guess we have to go up there."

"Is that where the money came from?"

"No, the one we're working on is where it came from."

The Sheriff bent down to Colton. "Can you show us where you found this money?"

"Yes, but there is no more, I took it all."

They headed upstairs to the main attic and Colton took them to where he had found the money. Jackson asked if he knew who put the money in there.

"You mean like did I see somebody put it in there?"

"Yes."

"No, I just found it. It was the money and the treasure. There were two guns too"

Jackson leaned down to his son and asked, "what two guns?"

"The ones in with the money."

"Where are the guns now?"

"I put them in the Sheriff's office down in Dodge City. I thought they would be safe there."

Jackson turned to the Sheriff. "I guess it's time to go down to Dodge City."

"What's Dodge City?"

Jackson took the Sheriff downstairs and over to the Dodge City's Sheriff office. He turned to Colton, "show us where you put the guns."

Colton walked over to one of the cells and pointed. "It's under the mattress."

The Sheriff put the two pistols in an evidence bag and they went back upstairs. Jackson smiled at Colton, "I think it's time that y'all go to on the bed."

"I'll take them." Sarah offered.

Jackson sat down at the table, he fiddled with the note and read it again. He couldn't believe what was happening. The Sheriff sat next to him, "It doesn't make any sense, Doc. I know this money and jewelry had to come from that robbery, but how did it get up in your attic? And who would put it there?"

"I don't know, but if this is what it takes to get Sandy back, I'll gladly turn it all over to them."

Chapter 30

Sandy studied the room that she was in. She wondered if she would be able to break the window to escape from it. She looked around for something that she could use that would help her. There wasn't much in here. She went to the dresser and opened each drawer. The top drawer held linens.

"Well, I can at least remake the bed."

The bottom two drawers were empty except for a tiny mouse who had scrambled away from her when she disturbed him. There was a small pile of nesting material in the corner of the drawer. Sandy opened the top drawer, took out one of the pillowcases, scrunched it up and left it in the mouse drawer.

She searched the entire room and the only thing she could come up with was a coat rod in the closet. She studied it carefully and thought she could probably dislodge it. She wondered if she would be strong enough to break the window with it. She would have to wait until it was quiet and they were asleep because she didn't know how much time it would take them to unlock the door to get to her.

~~~

Amanda had fallen asleep at the side of the road, she hadn't slept much in the last week between working, and being on alert in case Paul pulled anything funny.

She was startled awake by a bright light flashing into the car window. There was a light knock on it and she rolled down the window. It was a sheriff's deputy.

"Are you all right, Miss?"
~~~

"Yes, I was just so tired that I had to pull over, I must've fallen asleep."

"You have a driver's license?"

Amanda produced her driver's license which Deputy Taylor studied and then handed back to her. "There's a motel about 3 miles up the interstate off of Route 12. It's very late so maybe you should stop there."

"What time is it?"

"Almost 1 AM."

"I have to get home."

"How far is home?"

"Only 10 miles, I'll be fine now."

"Would you like me to follow you?" Deputy Taylor asked as he shined the flashlight into her back seat to make sure that she was alone.

"No, I'm sure I'll be fine, thank you."

"Good night, ma'am."

As Deputy Taylor walked back to his sheriff's car everything started running through Amanda's mind. She realized that Paul and Alvin were not going to let Savanna Shepard live. They would have no conscience about killing a little nine-year-old child. She knew she wasn't the best person in the world, but she was no child killer.

Amanda bolted out of her car and ran to the sheriff's car screaming. Deputy Taylor had just pulled back onto the road but came to a dead stop when he heard her. He got out and hurried over to her.

~~~

Sandy didn't know what time it was, but the tall, thin man they called Paul, had put a tray of food on the floor for her, a few hours ago. It laid untouched by the dresser and he never came back for it.

She was pulling the clothes rod down from the closet when she heard the key in the door. Quickly, she placed the rod on the floor as far back against the wall as she could. She hoped that he wouldn't see it. She just made it to the bed and sat down when the door opened.

"I brought you some more food, I hope you like hamburgers. It's our specialty tonight, and I got you a chocolate shake to go with it."

Sandy didn't say anything to Paul. She hadn't talked to any of them since they had taken her from the school.

"Okay, then, enjoy."

After Paul left, she went over and looked at the burger. It was not only greasy, but it was cold. She didn't trust that they wouldn't put something in the chocolate shake to make her sleep."

"Ick."

Sandy waited, but they never came back for this tray either. It got quiet, but she needed to wait longer. Finally, she crept over and put her ear to the door. She could hear nothing, not even the constant noise from the television. She went down on hands and knees to look under the door. All she could see were shoes kicked carelessly aside, a worn rug, and something blue that she couldn't identify.

Very slowly she shoved the dresser over toward the door. It made a scratching sound across the floor that sounded to her like it
~~~

had been amplified 20 times the actual sound. She cringed with each scrape thinking they would burst through the door at any moment. She managed to get the dresser all way across the door and everything remained quiet, no one came. She didn't want to stop when she started to push the dresser because she didn't know if she would have the courage to continue again. The dresser might give her the extra few minutes she needed.

Sandy backed away from the door like it was a snake ready to attack. She stood petrified to the spot. She waited, listened, but still heard nothing. When she finally got up enough courage she went to the closet and retrieved the pole. It was time to try to escape.

~~~

Deputy Taylor drove Amanda back to Dr. Shepard's house. The Sheriff answered the door. Jackson, Sarah, Sheriff Dustin and Deputy Rance Longman were sitting around the table waiting for Amanda to finish her story. She told him everything she could, and even confessed to killing her mother and her nasty brother, Bobby Joe so many years ago.

"Where exactly is this apartment?" The Sheriff asked.

The entire Sheriff's Department surrounded Paul's apartment. Jackson was waiting outside by the sheriff's car, Sarah had wanted to come also, but someone had to stay with the children and Jackson didn't want her in any danger. He would go with them, but the Sheriff wouldn't let him go any farther than the car.

Sheriff Dustin pounded on the door. Paul answered, saw the uniforms and shouted to Alvin. Paul was quickly secured; Alvin ran out of the bedroom with his pistol and shot randomly. He wounded both Deputy Adams and Deputy Coleman. Deputy Adams was wounded in the left leg and it would be six months before he would be able to return to duty. Deputy Coleman was grazed by another
~~~

bullet and he would require 12 stitches in his left arm. He returned to work in a month.

The other victim was Paul. He was hit by two of his brothers' bullets, one in the abdomen and the other in the neck. He died before he even hit the floor.

They were killed when the Sheriff and his deputies returned fire. Alvin died at the scene; he had been hit seven times.

Jackson couldn't stand it any longer, he bolted running into the house. Sheriff Johnny Dustin grabbed him and shouted, "she's not here. She's not here."

"What?"

"Sandy's not here, Jackson. We searched the entire house and it looks like she escaped. There's a broken window in one of the bedrooms. There's also blood but we don't know whose it is. We'll find her. I already have deputies on it."

Jackson looked around and nodded, he went over to help the injured deputies. In the distance they could hear sirens.

Chapter 31

Jackson continued to pace, there had been no word on what happened to Sandy. They had followed the blood path until it disappeared. The Sheriff called Morton Jack's to bring his big brown bloodhounds, Sundance and Babe to try to find Sandy's trail.

Jackson had given them a shirt of Sandy's that was in the laundry. Mort let the dog smell the shirt and they took off. Sheriff told Jackson to stay at home and he would call when found her.

Sheriff Dustin rang the Twilight Zone bell. He looked down at the little girl holding his hand. She giggled, "I hate that bell."

Jackson and Sarah opened the door.

"Daddy." Sandy yelled and threw herself into his open arms. He hugged her and kissed her; Sarah joined holding Sandy tight.

"Sarah, I really need a bath."

Sarah laughed. "Let's run up and get you one, and then we can wake your brothers."

While Sarah and Sandy were attending to her bath the Sheriff explained what happened. "Sundance and Babe found Sandy curled in a ball by the edge of the Schiller Woods, it's about 3 miles from Paul's apartment.

Sandy escaped by pulling the dresser in front of the bedroom door; they had locked her in. The room was empty except for the bed. She found a pole in the closet, took it down and broke the window and that's how she cut her arm. I ran her over to Jefferson Memorial and they put in 15 stitches. She is one brave little girl.

After the Sheriff left, Sandy told them the same story. Jackson gently took her hand. "Does your arm hurt?"

"A little, but it's okay."

"Are you alright?"

"Now that it's all over and I'm home. What about Paul and Alvin? Where are they?"

"They were killed by the Sheriff and his deputies."

Before Sandy could ask any questions, Stormy came tearing into the room and leapt at her. She went down on her knees and hugged the dog. Once they were settled again Jackson explained to her about Amanda.

She shook her head. "Amanda was my ghost?"

"Actually, the second one, the first was Lisa."

"What will happen to Amanda?"

"She'll probably spend some time in jail for her participation in your kidnapping."

Sandy went over and sat on her daddy's lap. "She's not really bad, she didn't want to do it. That Paul guy, he made her because he was mean to her and threatened her all the time."

"That will all come out court."

"What about Amanda's baby?"

"He's in a foster home with a very nice couple. They are petitioning the courts to adopt him. He'll have a very good home with them."

"I'm glad he'll have a place."

"Hey Sandy!" Lucas yelled from the stairs. He and Colton ran over and hugged her. "Are you okay? I looked all over for you at school."

"Was it awful?" Colton wanted to know.

"The only thing that was awful was not knowing if I would ever see any of you again. I was really scared."

Lucas grinned "you don't have to be afraid anymore, the ghosts are gone and so are the secrets of this house. Your home and we won't ever let you get away again."

If you enjoyed reading this book, try these other books:

by J. W. Becker

Flow River Series:

Returning to Flow River and Murder

Hannah's Secret

Greed, Money, and Murder

Murder at 3 P.M.

The Death of Travis McKenna

Deadly Lies   True Intent

A Time of Waiting

The Forever Series:

Book #1   Dust, Bones, and the Forever

Book #2   Journey toward the Forever

Book #3   Running into the Forever

Book #4   Dead Is Forever

Book #5   Returned to Evil

Ghost Stories:

Murder of a Ghost

Murder of a Blue Lady

Westerns:

The Captives: The Story of Wasser Thomas

Trail of Destiny: The Joseph Lansing Story

Comanche: The Martin McCoy Story

Single Books:

Time to Play the Game and Count the Dead

Shadows from the past

The Truth Is Always at an Angle

Step into Darkness

Shadows in the Darkness

Something Evil Follows

1918 When the World Shook with Fear

Good Child Bad Child Wrong Child

Th House That Held Secrets

Children's Books:

Welcome to Halloween

Christmas: A Special Time of Year

Stories from My Childhood

The Missing Angel

The Santa Letter

The Santa Sack

The Santa Sleigh

To the readers of my books:

I would like to thank you for reading my books. To me each one of these books represents something special, they are a part of me. I hope that everyone who has taken the time to walk through these books, enjoys them as much as I did when I wrote them.

You can only start an adventure with the first word written. Enjoy everything you read because whether you realize it or not, it is always a learning experience. Sit back and enjoy your time in someone else's world.

With my warmest regards,

J. W. Becker